Talking Bull

Talking *Bull*

AN INTERRACIAL CUCKOLD TALE

ROB MATTHEWS

fanny press

fanny press

A Fanny Press book published by Epicenter Press

Epicenter Press
6524 NE 181st St.
Suite 2
Kenmore, WA 98028
For more information go to: www.epicenterpress.com

Talking Bull
2020 © Rob Matthews

ISBN: 9781603816052 (trade paper)
        9781603816076 (ebook)

Printed in the United States of America

bull (bŭl) – *noun*

1. an uncastrated male cow, used for breeding
2. talk that is untrue or exaggerated
3. a sexually dominant man who cuckolds married or attached men for pleasure or profit

'Hello, Daniel Grant speaking.'

The man at the other end of the line coughs and clears his throat before stammering, 'Oh, hello … is Daniel Grant there, please?'

I smile to myself. A lot of people are on edge when they phone me for the first time. Writing a script in advance makes them feel less nervous, and they don't like deviating from it. 'Yes, that's still me,' I say, patiently.

'Yes, you did say, sorry. My name's Andy. I'm engaged—'

'Mazel tov.'

He laughs briefly. 'I'm engaged to Jenna. We're friends of Paula.'

This makes me sit up straighter. I wouldn't say any friend of Paula's is a friend of mine, but he does at least deserve attention.

I've been seeing Paula for two years, and I have a lot of time for her. I like Ray, her husband, as well. You might expect a bull to have contempt for cuckold husbands, but I've never thought like that. For me, it's just another sexual preference. I won't judge you for being straight, gay, bi, or trans. Spanker or spankee – your choice. If you're a man who wears ladies' underwear, I hope it feels good against your skin. If you're a cuckold, pleased to meet you: we can do business together.

Whenever I go to Paula and Ray's place, they have the kettle on. We've been known to spend an hour chatting over coffee before we get around to anything else. They're keen travelers, with stories to tell about temples in Bali and lagoons in Iceland. This goes on until one of them says, 'Shall we go upstairs and … get started.' As a euphemism for "fuck," I suppose "get started" is as good as any.

Walking through their bedroom door is like going on stage. From that moment, we're in character. Paula's the hot wife, who despises her pathetic husband. I'm the bull, there to get laid and to hell with everything else. Ray is the pleading cuckold, begging me to satisfy his wife because he can't. Sitting on a chair – carefully positioned for the best possible view – he says, 'Kiss her. She needs to be kissed by a real man.'

Generally, cuckolds stay fairly quiet during the sex. It's hard to talk if you're hyperventilating from excitement. If the cuck tries to include himself in the action, he might interject the occasional, 'She's gorgeous, isn't she?' Depending on what I'm doing at that moment, I'll respond or not. Ray is an exception. He keeps up a flow of comments and advice all the time I'm fucking his wife and seems to enjoy being acknowledged and ignored equally.

With mouths wide open, Paula and I lock our tongues together and kiss, passionately, aggressively. I unbutton her blouse. Her tits are so small and firm she never wears a bra. It's one thing I don't like about her, but I'll go into that later. I bend down to put my lips around one of her hard, pink nipples. 'They're beautiful, aren't they?' says Ray. 'Too good for me. She's *way* out of my league.' I undo the fastening on her trousers. They fall to the floor and she steps out of them. Ray says, 'Tell me you like her knickers. I bought them for her. Top of the range.' This can be my cue to rip them to shreds. But normally, she slides them down her legs and stands before me, naked. Only now do I remove *my* clothes. Taking off my shirt reveals taut black skin stretched over well-toned muscles and tightly curled chest hairs. I always flex my biceps and pop my pecs as I'm doing this. It makes Paula purr with lust. Ray moans, mainly with jealousy but there might be desire mixed in – who knows? When I get my cock out, Ray's pleas become more desperate. 'Please fuck my wife with your big, black dick. Mine's too small for her. Only you have what she needs.' She loves running her hands over my cock, enjoying how big and hard I am for her. She's not a huge fan of cock-sucking, which is fine: not everyone is. On the occasions when she does it, I suspect it's for Ray's benefit. His moans get more high-pitched as he watches his wife putting her lips around the head of my cock. But, usually, when she's finished touching me, she stretches out on the bed. There's no need for any more preamble. Handling my cock makes her wet enough. As for me, well, she has shoulder-length chestnut hair, deep brown eyes, and a good body. I have a solid erection every time I'm with her.

I always make sure I appreciate the moment when Paula, or anyone else, is lying on the bed, waiting for me. I honestly don't know how many women I've fucked in my life. You might assume it's in the thousands, but it's a more modest figure than that. I would guess around a hundred and fifty. I still find it overpoweringly erotic to see a naked woman lie down, open her legs, and give me a look that says, *I want you – now!* If I ever get blasé about that, it'll be time for this bull to go out to pasture.

As I lie on top of Paula, I barely hear Ray saying, 'Get your cock inside her. It's so much better than mine.' I'm concentrating on what I have to do. A true bull prides himself that his cock finds the entrance to a cunt – first time, every time. We leave the fumbling about while she says, 'Up a bit, left a bit,' to the cuckolds. I feel the hole with my finger once. That's enough for me to remember where it is. I replace my finger with the tip of my cock and push myself forward in one easy motion. Even a seasoned hot wife like Paula gasps at the sudden feeling of fullness when I'm inside her. She tells me – or, more accurately, tells Ray – how my cock stretches her pussy and gives her sensations no man has ever given her before. I take a second to enjoy her moist heat. This is the last time I focus on *me* until the end. For now, I'm like a poker player, watching for any changes in her breathing or facial expression, listening for every moan, groan, gasp, and sigh. Even though Paula's a regular, and I've never failed to make her cum, I don't get complacent. I watch her as closely as I do anyone I'm fucking for the first time. If you pay attention, a woman will always tell you what you need to do. When her breathing quickens and she moans loudly, keep doing what you're doing. When she goes quiet or you spot even a fleeting look of annoyance or boredom in her face, it's time to mix it up. It's not difficult, and I'm surprised every man hasn't worked it out yet. I can even read a cunt. From the way it expands and contracts around me, I know when I need to change the angle or the pressure. I do whatever's necessary to get her body and mind into the right state. Once she's there, I have only one goal.

Now, I've read the same stuff you have. *A woman can enjoy sex even if she doesn't have an orgasm.* That's like saying you can still enjoy golf if you knock the ball around for a while but never get it in the hole. Women love orgasms as much as men do. If she tells you she's satisfied without one, she's really saying your technique is so poor it'll take you all night to get her there and she has an early start tomorrow. I've also read that many women find it impossible to reach orgasm through intercourse. That's just to make you feel better, guys. *I've* never met a woman who didn't cum while I was inside her. Maybe I've been lucky a hundred and fifty times in a row, but I don't think so. I simply know what I'm doing.

Paula's breathing becomes deeper and faster as she gets close. This is when I need to be at my most focused. It's natural for a man to be excited in the presence of a sexually ecstatic woman. But forget about your own pleasure until later. I imagine a protective shell covering my cock, turning it into an insensitive rod. Its only job is to hit *her* nerve endings as often as it takes for her to cum. Paula's nostrils dilate as her mouth opens wide and the volume of her moans increases. Sweat glistens on her forehead. She goes rigid and her vaginal muscles clamp themselves around my cock. This lasts three seconds before her upper body jerks upward. I sometimes have to move out of the way to stop her head from smacking me in the face. Her moans become a scream as the orgasm takes over her body.

Afterwards, she goes limp. Her head flops down on the pillow. She doesn't move. It's as if all the life has been fucked out of her. Slowly, a smile spreads over her face and becomes a grin of pure happiness. Looking at me, she gives a nod, which means, *Your turn.* Now I can concentrate on my own pleasure. With Paula, I take that pleasure quickly. With other women, I go slowly, and before I reach my orgasm, they're halfway to a second one. It's impolite to leave them stranded in the middle, so I focus on them again. I'm not looking for sympathy: I have no objection to giving women multiple orgasms. But that's not Paula and Ray's thing. Once she's cum, they want me to finish the job as swiftly as I can.

They like me to ejaculate *on* her. Paula waves her hands vaguely around the area she wants me to target. Her stomach is a popular place. I'm not sure why Ray gets so excited if he sees I've filled her bellybutton, but he can discuss that with his therapist. She's also been known to turn over so I can shoot my load on her ass. But what they love most is when I cum on her tits. I crouch on the bed beside her. She grabs my cock and tugs it. I have big balls which hold a lot of semen. I fire a diagonal stripe of cum over both her tits. I've always got at least two further shots inside me, so I make sure each breast takes one full in the nipple. Her chest is well-covered by the time I'm done.

Knowing it's his time now, Ray stands up. That means I have to go. I put my clothes on and head out with a minimum of fuss. They trust me to let myself out, so I leave them to it. Ray is often on top of her before I'm out of the room. She kisses him passionately and says, 'Did you enjoy that, baby? Watching your naughty, slutty wife getting fucked.' Another of her favorites is to pull his face down to her chest and say, 'Smell the black man's semen on your wife's tits.' He usually does more than smell it. I often walk downstairs to the sound of him licking up my seed.

The leaving is another part I don't like so much about visiting Paula and Ray. I know I've chosen a lifestyle that doesn't involve a lot of cuddling. However, it would be nice if they'd at least acknowledge me on my way out. But she's teasing him about what she's done. He's doing what he can to claim her back. I shouldn't complain. A lot of guys would love the luxury of walking away straight after sex. But I always feel a twinge of sadness as I head down the stairs and hear Paula and Ray wrapped up in each other.

But, paradoxically, this is also what I like about them. I respect that they're a strong couple. I love the way they're both into the lifestyle. Ray looks forward to my visits as much as she does. He's hard from the moment I start undressing her, and I often notice him drawing his hand away from his cock as he's watching me in bed with his wife. He's so turned on, there's a danger he'll cum too soon and he doesn't want to spoil his turn with Paula after I'm gone.

'What did Paula say?' I ask Andy.

'That you've helped them and that … you might be able to help us too.'

'I'm sure I can. Talk to me, my friend.'

'Well, we've had this fantasy ....'

Of course, you have, I think. There comes a time in every relationship when one partner asks, 'What's your fantasy?' This is a stressful moment, because you *must* say the right thing. And that's very different from telling the truth. If the guy says, 'I would love to watch you make out with your sister,' that's it, the relationship is over. As for the woman, she knows how fragile the male ego is. If she admits to a crush on some film star, her partner could storm out, shouting, 'I'm not going to be anyone's second choice. If you want Channing Tatum, go and get him.' It's less risky to keep the fantasies as bland as possible. Clothes are generally uncontroversial. While it might raise eyebrows if you have a fetish for diapers or Nazi uniforms, you're safe with, 'I want you all in leather,' or, 'Why don't you wear black, lacey underwear?' But there's a problem. Once you've put the fantasy clothes on, it's difficult to have sex unless you take them off again. So, what was the point? These fantasies are a good place to start, but they only take you so far. Soon, you'll have to admit there are thoughts in your head that can't be satisfied with a trip to the fancy dress shop.

However, at this stage, the couple's clear on one thing: *It's all about you and me, honey.* Loyalty to each other takes precedence over everything. So, their fantasies begin with, 'I'd love it if *you* ...' or, 'What I want *you* to do to *me* is ....' But, as the relationship moves beyond the prelude, both of them grow in confidence, and there's the occasional hint that there might be people in the world besides the two of them. One of them says, 'Wouldn't it be hot if we did it outside, knowing someone could catch us at any moment?' As soon as they agree that they're open to *any* involvement of other people, it can escalate quickly. This is when some couples take their first, tentative steps down the path of cuckoldry.

One time, when they're in bed, the man suggests, 'Let's go to a bar and you can wear a low-cut top. You score a point for every guy who checks out your cleavage.'

Maybe she counters with, 'How would you like to watch me dancing with someone else? You can sit at a table while I throw shapes on the dance floor. Imagine how you'd feel if you saw me flirting with another guy?' If her partner none too discreetly touches himself at this thought, she'll up the stakes. 'What if he puts his arms around me and I look at you over his shoulder as we slow dance – my body tightly pressed against his?'

'How would you like it if he stole a kiss from you?' he asks, putting his lips against hers to illustrate the point.

If she returns his kiss passionately, the next step is pretty much inevitable. She draws her head back to look at him, bites her lip, and asks shyly, 'Would you like to watch me … do a bit more than kissing?'

Only one thing's going to happen now. He's going to fuck her harder than ever before. It'll be short, but it will be intense. Afterwards, there are nervous giggles or guilty looks. Both of them want to know, *Do you still love me now I've admitted to these thoughts?* They often say, 'Obviously, it's only a fantasy,' and, 'I would never dream of doing anything like that for real.' He's just cum and is in that brief post-coital period where love is more important to a man than sex. He says, 'It's best if we don't talk about that again.' She agrees and they move on with their day.

By the next time they're in bed, the urge has crept up on them again, so they negotiate a temporary waiver. 'Let's talk about it one more time. We'll get it out of our system and then never mention it again.'

Of course, they do mention it again – a lot. It becomes part of their sex routine. They go upstairs, undress, turn the light off, kiss, touch, and talk about her with other men. But, at this point, the men they talk about are archetypes rather than real people. She says, 'I was in bed with this big, strong guy,' or, 'This older man was fucking me – giving me the benefit of his experience, if you know what I mean.' She might choose a type who's an enhanced version of her partner. If he's blond and muscular, she'll tell him her lover was blond*er* and *more* muscular, sending the message, *He was like you – only better.* Other times, she fantasizes about a man who's the polar opposite of her partner. If he's a redhead with paper-white skin, she'll say she was with a black guy. This sends a different message; *You don't have what it takes to turn me on. I need another man for that.*

Every hot wife or girlfriend has her own idea of the right stud for her. Dark or fair, smooth or hairy, young and eager, or old and knowledgeable. But all imaginary bulls have one thing in common. No woman has ever taunted her partner by saying, 'I was in bed with this gorgeous stud. He had a half-inch dick and lasted ten seconds.' For her partner to feel the true cuckold emotions, he must hear, *In the most fundamentally masculine way, this guy was superior to you.* She might tell him plainly, 'His cock was bigger than yours.' But if she takes a subtle approach, she lulls him into a false sense of security by beginning, 'His cock was about the same size as yours.' But she gives an evil smile as she delivers the kicker, 'It was a whole lot *better*, though. It looked better, tasted better, and felt so much better inside me.'

When they start talking about cuckoldry, couples have a rule – spoken or unspoken – that they don't include people they know. It seems disrespectful to a friend if you make him the leading player in your fantasy. It's hard to look him in the eye if – unbeknownst to him – he fucked you from behind and called you a cum dumpster only the night before. But this line *will* be crossed. However seriously a woman takes her job, she can't simply turn off her outside interests the moment she gets to the office. She's going to notice the hot young salesman with his confident demeanor and smooth line of patter. Part of her enjoys being told what to do by her boss and she wonders if he's dominant elsewhere. The people around her will feed into her fantasies and she'll want to share these with her partner.

This is a natural progression, for the simple reason that everything's more exciting if it involves real people. If you heard one of your friends had made a porn film, you *would* seek it out. It wouldn't matter if you were attracted to that person or not. It's the same with fantasies. There's a limit to how many times you can get excited by a generic man in your bed. After a while, you have to put a face on him. The first step is to use celebrities. By now, the woman knows that her partner's as much into this as she is. His libido has long since shouted down his ego. So, she's free to imagine her favorite film star or singer fucking her. But it's difficult to suspend disbelief. If you live in a small flat in East London, what are the odds that Chris Hemsworth or Ryan Gosling's going to come knocking? If you like plausibility in your fantasies, you're going to talk about people you know. She says, 'I've always fancied your friend, John. When he was wearing those tight shorts last weekend, I could see how big he is. I would *love* to put my lips around your friend's big, hard cock. And I've seen him looking at my chest. That's when I lean forward to give him a better view. But I know how much he wants to see everything I've got. Imagine me showing my tits to your friend. These tits you love so much, baby. Think of John touching them and kissing them and sucking my nipples. Then I'm going to show him my cunt. When I say that, I don't mean letting him see my bush. I mean spreading my legs and opening myself up so he can see my lips and all the way up my wet, willing fuck hole.'

It feels wrong – and hence a hundred times hotter – to have fantasies about a friend. That's because it's so much more real. This is a person they know. So, what they're talking about *could* happen.

The stage of fantasizing but not actually doing anything can last three weeks or thirty years. It often lies dormant while the man and woman occupy themselves with little matters like building a career, getting married, and having children. For many couples, their journey will never get beyond this stage.

But, for others, that fateful night arrives, when they take the penultimate step. Maybe they're still a young boyfriend and girlfriend. Or perhaps they're a middle-aged married couple. The children have left home and she asks him one night, possibly as they're opening their third bottle of wine, 'Remember all that naughty stuff we used to talk about, back in the day? Do you think we might … possibly … someday … do something about it … you know … in real life?'

If he's got his rational head on, he'll be cautious. 'I always thought it was just words. Why, do *you* think we will?' But if he's recklessly drunk and horny, he'll say, 'Sure! Why not?'

They talk about cuckoldry. They've discussed it before, but this time, it's different. They talk about the *logistics* of her having sex with another man. One advantage of fantasy men, is they appear out of the ether whenever they're summoned. But if you want a real one, you have to find him from somewhere. The language the couple uses is not the same as in previous talks. She doesn't tease her partner by telling him how much better the other guy is. Nor does she try to excite him with crude language. She doesn't say, 'He's going to put his big cock in my wet cunt and fuck me so hard!' Their conversation is serious. Should they give their real names or invent *noms de sexe*? Is it safe to bring him back to their place or wiser to check in to a hotel? But the talk is more erotic than ever, because this fantasy might become reality.

Maybe he reckons they can go to a bar. If they sit apart, it won't be long until she attracts male attention. Some random guy comes up to her and asks if he can buy her a drink. But what's he going to say when he finds she's there with her partner? It's *possible* he'll say, 'That's cool. I'm happy to fuck you while he watches.' However, that's a bit of a long shot. He might freak out and cause an embarrassing scene. He could even get violent if he feels he's being played.

They've heard about swingers' clubs, but she says they can't go there. She has already made it clear they're *not* swingers. There was one evening when she drained her glass and told her partner, 'Here's the deal, sweetheart. I can have sex with as many men as I like. Nothing is off-limits. I'm going to kiss them passionately and let them explore every inch of my body. I can do oral, vaginal, anal – whatever I please. I'm going to let guys cum on my tits, in my face, and in my hair. But if you so much as hold another woman's hand, I'll never speak to you again.' He knows this is monstrously unfair. What he doesn't understand is why this unfairness turns him on so much. But he agrees a swingers' club isn't for them.

Ultimately, they're people of the modern world, so they turn to the internet. Firing up their laptop, they look at cuckold dating sites. They might content themselves with browsing the first time. Or they might throw caution to the wind and create a profile for her. He takes photos of her lying on the bed in bra and panties. In one, she has her hands behind her head. It's a pose that says, *Here are my armpits. Even though you can't smell them in a photo, take my word these are pheromone faucets. My pheromones are aimed at you, stud!* In another, she bites her finger in a way that's supposed to look both seductive and innocent. In all of them, she pushes out her breasts and sucks in her stomach. He enjoys taking the photos. Encouraging his girl into a variety of sexy poses feels good. Every cuckold has submissive elements in his makeup, but there's a hint of power reversal as he tells her, 'Lift your leg. Look at the camera like you want to ride it. Hold the underside of your boobs and offer them to the viewer.' He enjoys being the photographer, in control of the shoot. But stronger than that is the thrill of making his woman sexy, so she'll be attractive to *someone who isn't him.*

Writing the profile is equally exciting. What should they include? Is this a good time to talk about her love of tennis and ballroom dancing, or should they focus on her penchant for being tied up and spanked? What do they say about the man they're looking for? Do they want to specify "tall, dark, and handsome," or are they afraid this will rule out the hot blond guys? And what about the age range? Is 18 to 30 too restrictive? The 18 is non-negotiable, but she might want to try her luck with an older guy.

When they're happy with the words and images, they press the *Submit* button, put the laptop aside, and have sex again. It's the most intense fuck they've had in ages.

When they wake up the next morning with throbbing heads and vile breath, there are two ways they can go. Maybe she says, 'Hey, babe, did we do anything stupid last night?' The realization that you've posted on a cuckold dating site is one of the best hangover cures out there. They both sit bolt upright, suddenly full of energy. Turning on the laptop again, they delete the profile, and breathe a sigh of relief. Nonetheless, she spends the rest of the day doing every internet search she can think of to make sure the photos of her drunk and trying to be sexy haven't gone viral.

The alternative is that he makes coffee and they lie in bed, slowly coming back to life. She says, 'You remember we placed an ad on cuckold.com? How do you feel about that now?'

He doesn't know what the right answer is, so he says, 'Er ... not sure. What do *you* think?'

For the first time that morning, her bloodshot eyes sparkle. 'I suppose there's no harm in leaving it there for the moment. It'll be fun to see if anyone replies. Who knows, if the right guy gets in touch ...?'

And then they discover the other best hangover cure is vigorous sex.

Afterwards, he has his first experience of the cuckold's mixed emotions. He'd better get used to them. He feels proud that his woman is confident in her ability to attract other men. At the same time, he's jealous because she *wants* to attract them. He wonders why he isn't enough for her. But as he recovers from his post-orgasm sadness, he realizes he's still massively turned on by the thought of his partner with another man. He can't explain why. All he knows is that his heart pounds more at the prospect of other guys fucking her than at the thought of doing it himself. This means he has the heart of a cuckold.

So, they wait and see what replies come in. Inevitably, they're disappointed. Guys on dating sites play the numbers game. I would too, if I were in their shoes. It's natural to feel annoyed if you spend an hour composing a witty and informative message to a woman, only to have her ignore it. But, if you go into the profiles of a hundred women and post, "How you doing?" or even just, "Sup?" there's a chance one or two will reply and you haven't wasted much time.

There are also the people who contact you, but only to chat. They're the reason I steer clear of cuckold dating sites these days. A few years ago, I created a profile on cuckold.com. A friend of mine had taken arty photos of me with my shirt off, so I used these to back up my claim that I was a well-toned black stud. The first guy who replied included a picture of his wife – or a woman he claimed was his wife – and told me she was desperate to meet a black man for sex. He wanted to know what would happen the first time she met me. I wrote back saying we'd get together for a drink and a chat. If things went well, we might take it further. He fired back his response, "Further in what way? What *exactly* would you do?" Nowadays, that would be enough for me to block him. Being less worldly-wise back then, I said we'd probably go back to their place and have sex. He persisted, "*How* would you have sex with my wife?" This back-and-forth continued for a week. I tried many times to steer the discussion round to when and where we'd meet, but he wasn't interested. He just wanted details about what I would do to his wife. It took me longer than it should have done to realize he had no intention of letting me meet her – if she even existed. He simply got off on talking about it.

But maybe the couple does find a man worth contacting. Messages are exchanged on the site. After a while, they risk giving him their email address. All the signs are positive. Finally, they send the momentous email giving a time and a place. He writes back, "See you there."

As soon as they read that, they go to bed. Neither of them shuts up for a second while they're having sex. He says, 'You're going to meet another guy and he's going to fuck you.'

She counters with, 'And you're going to watch him fucking me.'

'Are you looking forward to it?'

'Oh, baby, it's all I can think about.'

'You are such a slut.'

'You're a pervert for wanting me to do it.'

'Sluts and perverts go well together, don't you think?'

'We deserve each other.'

'Close your eyes and imagine him fucking you right now.'

She shuts her eyes, smiles ecstatically and calls out the name of the guy they're going to meet. This causes her partner to cum instantly. It's the one time in her life she's turned on by premature ejaculation.

It's still a fantasy they can enjoy in the security of their own bed. Even now, it's not certain anything will happen. As the day approaches, she might get scared but dismisses it as pre-show jitters. On the night itself, she's put on the underwear they bought specially for the occasion. He's zipped up the little black dress for her. She's applying her makeup when she slumps down on the bed and says, 'I don't think I can do this.'

He puts his arm around her and says, 'What's wrong, babe? You were so excited about hooking up with this guy.'

She looks at him sadly and says, 'I know, but you and I love each other. What were we thinking, inviting someone else into our relationship?'

He checks that she's sure. Part of him is disappointed but another part is relieved. He sends an email saying, "Sorry. Family emergency. We've got to cancel." And they have a quiet evening in. They eat pizza, drink wine, and watch a movie. They might try again another time or resign themselves to a life that's a lot less exciting but a whole lot safer.

For other people, reality bites a bit later. She gets herself ready. He reassures her that she looks fantastic. They hold hands in the taxi. He asks if she's excited. She doesn't say anything but nods as enthusiastically as she can. They arrive at the meeting place. Maybe the other guy has got there first. She looks through the window and sees a real, flesh and blood man waiting for them. He's there for one reason: he wants to fuck her. She might suddenly think there's something predatory about him. He uses attached women for sex. It's all too much. She says, 'I've got to get out of here,' and turns on her heel. Her partner uses text rather than email to report the family emergency.

But, they might go in and meet him anyway. One reason could be simple politeness. After all, this guy has made the effort to come out and see them. It would be rude to stand him up. Or there might be a part of her that's still intrigued, despite her fears. The three of them sit down together. They have a drink or a bite to eat, and her nerves settle. The man she's getting to know undergoes another transformation. She discovers there are ordinary-person things about him. He has dreams, problems, a family, friends, a job – everything she has. She might even find – shock horror – that she likes him.

My advice to all bulls meeting a couple for the first time is: be nice! Don't go in shouting, 'Suck my cock, bitch,' or, 'Beg me to fuck her, wimp.' These may be appropriate things to say later, but get to know the couple first. Remember they're people. You may be aiming to have an unusual relationship with them, but you are still creating a relationship. So, buy them a drink. Ask about their day. Discover what they want to get out of the experience. If they trust and like you, it increases the chances of them letting you into their lives and their bed.

The downside of this could be that the three of them are getting on so well she forgets what brought them together in the first place. If they like the same music or films, they could chat away happily with no mention of sex. Her partner's usually the one to remind her, because he's getting confused. They came here to fulfil their cuckold fantasies, but all he sees is people having a pleasant conversation. He tries to get the evening back on track by asking a blunt question like, 'So, what do you think of her? Good enough for you?' She and the stud exchange a discreet eye-roll. This is the start of a bond between them that is separate from the one she has with her partner. After that, she and the stud call the shots between them, and move it along as *they* see fit. He might go with, 'This place is getting too noisy. Perhaps we should go somewhere a bit more quiet.'

Or maybe she'll pull a face and say, 'This wine doesn't take any prisoners. We've got much better stuff in the fridge. Why don't we head back to ours?'

Regardless of how they dress it up, they're saying, 'Let's go someplace where we can be intimate.' She might be curious about what it would be like to kiss him. Maybe he wants to sit closer to her and inhale her feminine scents. They could want to gaze into each other's eyes with an intensity that doesn't feel comfortable in a public place.

So, they get up and leave. Even now, it's not a done deal. The woman still has to overcome the shock of the first intimate touch. Up to now, she and the bull have been chatting and laughing together. She's put her hand on his arm a couple of times to emphasize a point. But, essentially, they've been interacting as friends. When they get to a private place, though, she thinks, *The talking's over. It's time for action.* An experienced bull takes gentle but firm control. He guides her to the couch, and sits her down. He kisses her – not aggressively, but assertively. And suddenly, there's a pair of lips on hers that aren't her partner's. Hands are touching her in a way that's different from normal. Maybe it feels weird and she has to call a halt. However, the alternative possibility is that her lips touch the bull's and she realizes they're *better* than her partner's. The touch of these new hands on her body is making her tingle in a way she hasn't experienced since she and her partner first got together. She kisses the stud back with an enthusiasm that makes her partner's jaw drop.

This *is* the point of no return. Only the roof falling in could stop these people from having sex now.

At this stage, there's often a change in the dynamic and it's the woman who pushes it along. A good bull will let this happen. This can be difficult for her partner to watch. He can't kid himself she's only letting this happen to please him. There's nothing passive about the way she takes the stud's hand and places it on her breast, inviting him to stroke and squeeze it. She pops open the buttons on his shirt and puts her hand inside. She wants to know if he's smooth or hairy. She also wants to feel a well-developed, manly chest. He sits quietly and lets her explore. He knows his body's giving her enough entertainment for the moment and he doesn't have to do anything else.

She slows down when it's time to reveal *her* body, looking shy as she takes off her top. No matter how confident she is about her appearance, this is a fraught moment for any woman. She's been part of a couple for some time, now. Security leads to complacency. Evenings spent watching TV and eating nachos can seem more appealing than hitting the gym. She's asking herself if she's still got it. Can she arouse a man who's not her partner?

I would reassure all women that they shouldn't be concerned about this when they're with a real bull. I've often been asked what sort of woman is my type. I reply that *all* women are my type. If you set out to be a bull, you can't say that you're only going to fuck women of a certain ethnicity or that you don't go for redheads. A stud must be omnivorous. I can find something appealing in any woman. I like blondes, brunettes, dark haired women, and redheads equally. A button nose is cute, but a prominent one gives a face character. Small breasts have large suckable nipples. But, there's nothing I enjoy more than burying my face in a pair of big tits. I appreciate the taut abdominal muscles of a gym-rat girl and also the soft, womanly roundness of a larger lady. The classic cuckold fantasy is that of a black man with a white woman, so I'm most in demand from white couples. But I've also fucked black and Asian women, and always found plenty to appreciate in them.

I find it hard to believe there are any guys who are attracted to just one type of woman. However gorgeous your blonde girlfriend is, you'll see a woman passing by with glossy, black hair and you'll ache for her. You've married a beautiful French seductress, but then meet a cute Asian girl. It doesn't matter how much you love the one you're with: you're always going to notice the others. Part of you will resent the fact that options have been cut off from you. I don't have that problem. If I'm with an Italian woman today, I might be with a Swedish woman tomorrow. This week's hot wife is deliciously chubby, but next week's will be slim and elegant.

So, ladies, if you're with a bull, don't worry when you take your clothes off. He *will* like your body. But, can I give you one piece of advice? If it's your first encounter with a stud – or, indeed, any man – be sure to wear a bra. You might think it makes a big impact when you pull off your t-shirt with a dramatic sweep and your tits are just there, in the guy's face. That's like revealing who the murderer is in the first scene of the movie. I'm not saying it never works, but it's usually better to let the suspense build. Especially when I'm with a married woman for the first time, I like the breasts to be revealed slowly. It's one of the illicit moments of intimacy that make cuckoldry so exciting, and I don't want to hurry it. Because, guys, I shouldn't know that your wife has large red areolae, or whether her nipples are pink or brown, or how hard those nipples get when they're tweaked. Only you should know this about her, and that turns you on. You love the way she reveals all those "private" parts of herself to a man who isn't you.

I like to tease myself by finding out all these details as slowly as possible. And this requires a bra, which is like gift wrapping – hinting at what lies beneath without giving too much away. I've seen a number of different bra types employed for this first reveal. A lot of women play it safe and go with standard ideas of erotic. The world has got it into its head that lacey equals sexy. However, lacey often means transparent and I prefer an opaque bra. If the woman's excited, her nipples will be poking through the fabric. This is a good enough preview. I like to hook two fingers into the left cup and pull it down slowly. This causes the boob to reveal its shape and show how round and full it is. The areola – or lack thereof – is the next to come into view. This is followed by the grand entrance of the nipple – the undoubted star of this part of the show. I love this process and I've asked Paula many times if she'd consider wearing a bra when I come round. She puts her hands to her chest and says, 'Nothing to support here.'

It's the same with panties. You cannot do without them. The slow revelation of the pussy is just as important. Cunts are, or at least should be, infinitely varied, and discovering a new one is always fascinating. This is done with tantalizing slowness if you're wearing panties. A few stray pubes emerging from either side of the gusset indicate a full bush. Women often beat themselves up if this happens, but why should they? A hairy cunt is sexy. Genital baldness is in favor these days. Don't get me wrong, I like a shaven pussy as much as the next guy. If you're genuinely eating a woman out, as opposed to licking her clit, it's easier if there's nothing in the way. You don't spend twenty minutes coughing up a hairball afterwards. But, declaring all pussies must be shaven is like saying all ice cream must be strawberry. Regardless of how much you love one thing, it's nice to have variety. Some I like better than others. I know the Brazilian has its fans, but, to me, it looks like you were careless when shaving and missed a bit. My least favorite is the postage stamp, especially on dark-haired women. I don't want to feel like I'm making out with Hitler when I go down on you. A regular bikini wax is okay. It's like pruning a tree to make it neater while preserving its essential treeness. Sculpting your pubes into a heart, an arrow, or a four-leafed clover is like calling your house Seldom Inn: amusing the first time but soon gets old. It's fine by me if you want to let your bush grow wild and untrammeled. It adds to the mystery if I have to find my way through the jungle to reach the treasure.

I'm told that shaving is becoming common amongst men these days. Sorry if that's what you like, ladies, but I'm not going there. I did try it once. A woman I was seeing thought it would be fun if we shaved each other. So, I took the rash step of letting a woman near my junk with a razor blade. I guess I trusted her. I thought I looked odd without pubes. It was like seeing someone without his wig for the first time. But she loved it and spent the next half hour licking and sucking around my cock and balls. I didn't complain about that but, as the hair grew back, the whole area itched like a bastard. It's not acceptable for a man to scratch his crotch at work so I had to look at my clients through watering eyes. When I got with another woman ten days later, she complained I was giving her crotch stubble rash. I was forced to take a vow of chastity until my pubes grew back and I told myself I'd never shave down there again. Apart from anything else, women like my manliness. Men are big. They are strong, and they are hairy. Women love to run their fingers across the stubble on my chin or down the tight curls on my chest. There is nothing manlier than a big, hard cock emerging from a thick bush of black hair.

But, going back to cunts. There's another thing I want to say about them. I know people often find this gross, so apologies in advance if I appall anyone. But I'm here to tell you the truth as I see it. Cunts smell. There, I said it. If I may elaborate a little, cunts smell great. I know women who spend all afternoon in the bath if they've got a date that evening. They also use douches, sprays, and pearls – doing whatever they can to eliminate the aroma. This is a mistake. If you want something with no smell and no taste, eat tofu. Cunts have a rich, complicated scent. Yes, it takes a bit of getting used to. But you thought Roquefort was disgusting the first time you tried it but soon learned to appreciate its complexity. And, guys, it's not like our cocks smell of fresh strawberries, so let's not take the high ground here. As I'm kissing and licking a pussy for the first time, I always inhale deeply, enjoying the specific notes that make it unique. I make sure her husband knows what I'm doing. It takes a special level of intimacy for me to know what his wife's cunt smells like. I want him to understand how well I know her.

In Shakespeare plays, they like to play the trick of slipping another woman into bed in place of the one the man expected. This wouldn't work with me, no matter how dark it was, because I could always tell the difference by the way she smelled. As soon as I kissed her cunt, I'd realize a switch had been made. Whether I'd *stop* is a different matter.

A good stud will always be complimentary about the woman on their first time together. However, many women *he's* had, this is a big moment for *her*. She's taking a risk, stepping outside the safety of her relationship. So, the bull must be supportive. A barely audible 'Wow!' or 'Beautiful!' will be enough, but he must make it clear that he appreciates what she's showing him. He needs to spend a long time touching, kissing, and looking at her breasts. Even if he thinks they're run-of-the-mill, he must act as if they're the most beautiful things he's ever seen. He needs to marvel at her cunt like it's the Venus de Milo and eat it with the enthusiasm of a starving man devouring a meat pie.

But, having said that, it must be remembered that a bull does not spend too long on cunnilingus. A cuckold licks a woman for hours on end because he knows it's the only way he can give her pleasure. For a stud, cunnilingus is an appetizer – an *amuse chatte*.

I want to say a few words to any of you guys who fancy yourselves as potential bulls. I'm all for equal opportunities, but this isn't something everyone can do. There are certain qualities you must have. The first is that you need to be reasonably well-endowed. You don't have to be John Holmes, but a stud with a two-inch dick is a contradiction in terms. Speaking for myself, I have a solid eight inches when fully erect. And I'm lucky enough that my cock doesn't shrink down to a button mushroom after I've cum. Even in repose, it shows its potential with five inches of good girth.

However, it's not enough to have the right tool: it needs to be in working order. You must be able to get hard. This can be difficult, especially the first few times another man is in the room with you. You're not used to having an audience, and this might throw you off your game. Unless the cuckold's caged or restrained, he's got his cock in his hand and is hugely excited by the scene playing out in front of him. It's an embarrassing role reversal if the cuck is hard while the so-called bull is floppy. If you find yourself saying, 'This has never happened before,' or, 'Shall we take a break and try again in twenty minutes?' you're not cut out to be a stud. Leave lines like that to the cuckolds.

The third quality you must have is staying power. A woman does not want a bull to make her cum with his tongue, his fingers, or a vibrator. After all, any man – even her partner – can do that. What she wants is for the bull to get his big, hard cock inside her and fuck her until she screams.

So, by all means, kiss and lick her cunt. Do this to give her pleasure and because you enjoy it. Taunt the cuckold with it. But, don't use it as a means of pushing her any appreciable way toward orgasm. That's what your cock is for.

Remember the stud is being brought in as an expert. Husbands call a plumber because he's better with the pipes and drains than they are. They call a bull because he's better at sex than they are. The sad truth is that husbands generally aren't good at fucking. That's not the basis on which they're selected. Guys, the chances are your wife's with you because you make her laugh or you're a steady provider. Maybe you're a great dad. That's more important to her in choosing a life-partner than sex. But she deserves good cock, so call in a specialist. You love her, so why wouldn't you want her to have the best?

She knows that's what she's getting as the bull throws her down on the bed and gets on top of her. Her mouth's open and her eyes are shining. Something special is about to happen. There's also a bit of apprehension or even fear. After years of predictable sex with her partner, she's worried about her match fitness. Is she ready for a stud?

When he sees her concern, he must offer reassurance, not with words, but by going slowly. His cock is bigger than her partner's – probably the biggest she's ever had. In time, she'll learn to love it when the bull rams his cock into her hard. When he's first with her, he should push forward firmly but gently. Give her cunt a chance to expand so she can accommodate a big, thick cock. With no fear of losing his erection, the bull can take his time. I've known studs who spend half an hour completing penetration. They go an inch inside her, make sure she's comfortable, and go in another inch. It takes patience as well as trust and communication, but it's worth it. She appreciates the care he's taking, and relaxes, knowing her body's in the hands of a master.

Women react in a variety of ways after their first experience with a stud. Some find the experience too intense and break down in tears. Others laugh at the sheer outrageousness of what they've done. Some say, 'I had no idea it could be like that,' and, 'I can't believe I waited so long to do this.' Then there are those who find it difficult to form a coherent thought and can only manage, 'That was … like … wow!'

But all women have this in common: they all want to do it again. Maybe they don't realize immediately. When the ecstasy of cumming fades, the woman might look over at her partner and say, 'That was wrong. We shouldn't have done that. Never again.' But this doesn't last. The guilt fades, leaving a desire that builds like an itch. I've yet to meet a woman who, in a state of calm rationality, says, 'Yes, that was nice, but once is enough for me.' This can be a problem for her partner. Maybe he had the idea that she could fulfil this fantasy one time and get it out of her system. But it doesn't work like that. In fact, the opposite is true. It gets it *into* her system. The difference between sex with a regular guy and with a bull is like that between an amateur singer and a professional. The first might offer a pleasant way of spending an evening. The second leaves you stunned with the talent on display. Now that she's experienced real sex, she's not going to be satisfied with the pale imitation offered by her partner. This isn't a cork that can be easily put back in the bottle. Because, fundamentally, it's what women need.

I sense a lot of people bridling when I say that. How dare I talk about what women need? I see your point. I'm sure I don't fit most official definitions of a feminist. But I am one, in my own way. I believe women should have the same opportunities as men in all walks of life, including sex. We live in a world where sex too often revolves around the man's pleasure and finishes when he ejaculates. However, a good stud is concerned primarily with the woman's pleasure. Sex with a stud can end when the *woman* cums. What a concept. Knowing that he's given her pleasure could be enough to leave *him* satisfied. There are times when I've arranged to fuck two women in one day. On these occasions, I make sure I don't cum when I'm with the first one. It's not that I can't perform after I've orgasmed: I've been known to fuck the same woman six times in one day with both of us cumming every time. But, I'm not at my absolute best if I've already cum and no woman deserves the second pressing of the grape. Each one should be serviced by a bull who is at the top of his game and giving his all.

I know all this because I have a lot of experience with hot wife and cuckold couples. I don't fly in, fuck the wife, and fly out again. I take the time to talk to them. All the couples I've met have gone down pretty much the same path. They might miss stops or add a few extra, but basically, it's the same journey for everyone.

So, I pretty much know word for word what Andy's reply is going to be but, nonetheless, I ask him, 'What fantasy?'

I also know he's not going to give me a straight answer. 'Jenna and I have been together five years. We're very much in love.'

'I'm happy for you.'

'We've always had a good sex life.' This is the time when a man will often tell me the size of his penis. Friends who have known him all his life have no idea of his length and girth and yet he reveals this information to a stranger on the phone. The reason is simple. What he's saying is, *I'm not like the other cuckolds. I don't have a one-inch dick.* Andy doesn't tell me this. He says another line I've heard before. 'We don't *need* this. It's something we *want* to try.'

'How old are you guys?'

'I'm 36. Jenna's 34.'

'That's good.'

'Yes, it's not a bad age to be,' says Andy. 'She's at her sexual peak. For me that was twenty years ago.' He chuckles self-consciously at this joke on God's part.

'What does Jenna look like?' I ask.

'Strawberry-blonde hair down to her shoulders, blue eyes. She's … put on a little weight recently, but she carries it well.' He can't see me, but I nod appreciatively it this. It's a good way of saying, *She's chubby, but I like it.* 'Her boobs have grown,' he adds, proudly. 'They're 36c now.'

'She sounds great,' I say.

He doesn't tell me what he looks like, guessing – correctly – that this doesn't matter. Instead, he asks, 'What about you?'

That *is* important. 'I'm 37. I'm fit and strong. I have two slabs of pectoral muscle and six pack abs. In short, I look the way a man is supposed to look. Jenna would get wet just from passing me in the street.'

He moans, reminding me of the noise Ray makes when he sees me naked. I always find it amusing when straight men are aroused by me. I'm not only the dream of married women: I'm the dream of a whole lot of married men, as well. 'Er … sorry to ask …' he says, 'but … do you charge for what you do?'

'Absolutely not,' I reply. Many people have suggested I could make a lot of money doing this. If you see a brilliant guitarist or footballer, it's natural to suggest they turn professional. I am highly-skilled in my chosen field, but I've never wanted money for it. I don't want to go into any sexual encounter thinking, *I've got to do this – it's my job.* There's a perverse part in a lot of people that makes us resent an activity as soon as we get paid for it. It becomes work, drudgery. For me, fucking a woman is its own reward. Yes, I focus more on her pleasure than mine, but I enjoy her orgasms as much as she does. The surge of satisfaction I get when I make a woman cum with my cock often matches the intensity of my own orgasm. 'Do you have any children?' I ask.

'No.'

This is good to hear. I hate it when couples say, 'Yes, we've got kids, but don't worry, they'll be asleep. They won't disturb us.' Childhood is hard enough without wondering why strange noises are coming from mummy and daddy's bedroom. What if junior has a nightmare and comes running in? Kids aren't stupid and they don't believe you when you say mummy has a sore back and this nice man is rubbing it to make her feel better. I fully support the right of mothers to have great sex. But, let's do it well away from the little ones and make sure it doesn't affect them. I hope this will count in my favor when I die and God reminds me that *Thou shalt not commit adultery* was a commandment, not a suggestion. I'll be able to say, 'I know, Lord, but at least I took steps to protect the children.' With luck, He'll beckon me in and introduce me to a couple of hot angels. But, while we're on the subject, I think there's a good chance God is up there saying, 'People, why are you so hung up on sex? There are more important ethical issues out there!' If you don't kill anyone, don't steal, treat people well, and are kind to animals, I think God will overlook what you do with your genitals.

Andy has passed the initial screening, so I ask him, 'Would you like to meet?'

He pauses. They often do at the moment when the fantasy suddenly gets very real indeed. 'Well ... if you want, we've got a nice place …. After all, you're a friend of Paula's. If you and Jenna get on well, you could ….'

'Let's go to a bar first,' I say, firmly.

Always meet a blind date in a public place is advice given to women, not six-foot men. But I insist on meeting in public the first time because it makes it easier to get out of awkward situations.

One time, years ago, I met a couple for the first time at their house. The man, Peter, was a bit *too* up for it. He shook my hand warmly as he invited me in. Millie, his wife, was sat on the couch, looking like she wanted to disappear into it. She nodded and gave me a wan smile, but didn't stand up. She had short, mousey hair, pale blue eyes, and a tiny nose. I'd have called her sweet-looking rather than sexy.

'I have to say, you are perfect,' said Peter. 'He really is the man of our dreams, isn't he, darling?'

Millie didn't say anything.

He continued, 'So, our fantasy is that you have sex with Millie in every room of the house. I hope you don't mind, but I want to take loads of photos. It's important for us that we have a record of this.'

'How do you feel about this?' I asked her.

'What, the photos?' she said, dully. 'I suppose it'll be okay. Even if they find their way onto the internet, who's going to notice me among millions?'

'I mean the whole business.'

Peter answered for her. 'Are you kidding? She's even crazier about it than I am. It's always been your fantasy, hasn't it, darling?'

She looked at the floor and said again, 'I suppose it'll be okay.'

For most guys, that would be the only green light they needed. Not for me. I don't want mere consent: I want enthusiasm.

'Of course, it will be okay,' he said. 'We're never going to find anyone better than Daniel, so why waste time? Now, I've been shopping. I've got marvelous toys and lots of lovely clothes for us all to wear. I'll go and get them.'

He ran up the stairs. As soon as he was out of earshot, I leaned into Millie. 'You don't want to do this, do you?'

She shook her head. 'No offense to you. If I met you on a girls' night out, I'd do you in a heartbeat. But the idea of my husband *wanting* me to do it and *watching* creeps me out. It's not normal, is it?'

'More common than you'd think. But, if you're not into it, I'll leave right now. And … Millie, I'm no marriage counselor, but if he forces you into places you don't want to go, you might want to think about leaving too.'

She gave me a look of such gratitude that I was tempted to take her with me. It would have been a great dramatic gesture in a movie. In real life, though, I wouldn't have had a clue what to do with her afterwards. I doubt she'd have been happy sleeping on my couch. I settled for kissing the top of her head. I was making for the door when Peter hurried down the stairs with two carrier bags full of his props. 'Where are you going?' he demanded.

I held up my phone. 'I got a text. My brother's in hospital. I've got to go.'

He dropped his bags and stood between me and the front door. 'You can't go until you've fucked Millie.'

Did this guy really think I could perform at my best while fretting over my brother, who was teetering between life and death? The fact that I don't have a brother is neither here nor there. Peter wasn't to know that. I'd conceived quite a dislike for him and knocking him to the floor would have been fun. I also had the feeling Millie would have enjoyed seeing that. But judges don't always accept, 'He was an asshole,' as compelling defense when you're facing assault charges.

As it was, she was the one who saved the day. 'He's leaving because of these,' she said. I turned to look at her. She'd unbuttoned her blouse and was showing her tits, which were small with nipples like little red berries. 'He took one look at these and decided I wasn't worth fucking.' I had a good idea what she was doing. She knew the ins and outs of Peter's sexuality better than anyone, whether she wanted to or not. Even so, part of me wanted to reassure her that she had nice tits and was totally worth fucking. She continued, 'He said these boobs were only good enough for a pervert like you, not a real man like him.'

He looked at me and I shrugged, in a way that could have been interpreted as either, *I've no idea what she's talking about* or, *What can I say, dude, I call it as I see it?* He took two steps toward her and asked, 'How did that make you feel?'

It was enough to give me a clear passage to the front door. I went straight out, giving Millie a thumbs-up over my shoulder as I left. Peter made no further attempt to stop me. He didn't get to see me fuck his wife, but he got to hear her talk about how the big, black stud had dissed her tits. That seemed to be a good enough consolation prize for him.

I never saw either of them again. I hope she's okay and that she's ditched him. But the point of this story is that, if Millie hadn't intervened, it could have been difficult for me to get out of the house. Since then, I've always met people in public the first time. I know a couple of bars that have seats secluded enough for a private chat but that also offer an easy escape route. There's one place I particularly like for initial meetings.

'Do you know Ophelia's bar?' I ask Andy.

'Yes,' he says. 'I'm coming along too. Is that okay?'

'More than okay – it's mandatory.'

I've learned how important it is to meet both the man and the woman before anything happens. Years ago, when I was a naïve young bull – scarcely more than a calf – I made the mistake of meeting only the female half of the couple. I thought it would be okay. After all, the two most important players were me and the wife. The husband would most likely be only a spectator.

She was called Julie. A glamorous woman in her early fifties, she had a bright smile and dark, wavy hair, which fell across her large breasts. Her eyes were a little too wide and the skin around them implausibly smooth, so I knew she'd had work done. She wasn't fat, but her hips and thighs had a womanly curve to them. As soon as I met her, my body responded. 'First of all, let me say that I am the luckiest woman in the world,' she began.

'You won the lottery twice?' I suggested.

'Even better than that. William is a wonderful man.' She paused and added, 'He's my husband.'

'I guessed.'

'He has a great job in the city, which means I don't need to work.'

It's all right for some, I thought, but immediately told myself not to be jealous. God doles out different gifts to different people. Some are smart, others are good-looking. Then there are those who are put into the path of a guardian angel who'll look after them. God gave me a large dick and a phenomenal capacity for bringing women to orgasm. I have nothing to be jealous about.

'Now the kids have left home,' she continued, 'we've decided to recapture that old magic in the bedroom. We started fantasizing in bed.' I smiled quietly as I waited to hear the usual. But she cut straight to, 'Our favorite is that he comes home from work one day and catches me in bed with a guy.'

This sounded like fun. 'You want me to be that guy?'

Her eyes roaming over my body, she said, 'Hell, yeah, I do. Are you free tomorrow evening? He gets home at six. If you come round at five-thirty, we can be in full flow by the time he arrives.'

We shook hands and I went home, excited about the following evening. I thought it could be erotic, maybe even funny. When he came in and caught us, it would be like an old bedroom farce. He might use a line like, 'How could you? This is what you get up to while I'm slaving away at work?' But he'd soon drop the pretense of being outraged and sit down to enjoy the show.

Everything still seemed on the up and up when I got to their place the next day. She answered the door wearing a black combination that looked difficult to put on. There was a gold buckle between the bra cups. Another one joined the bra to a see-through section that covered her belly. This was linked to her stockings by suspenders. There was a good eight inches of bare thigh above each stocking top. As I walked in, she grabbed my shoulders and pulled me toward her. She kissed me. She had nice lips, full and sensual. Her hand went down to my crotch and she gave my cock a gentle squeeze through my pants. 'No one's going to be disappointed today,' she said. She took my hand and started to lead me upstairs.

I wanted to check the arrangements first. 'Have you heard from William? Is he on his way?'

'He'll be here soon,' she said.

'Is there anything he especially wants to see when he gets in? Any particular position? Or is he leaving it up to you?'

'It's all up to me.'

We went up to their spacious bedroom. A king-sized bed dominated the center of the room. Her outfit might have been difficult to put on, but was surprisingly easy to take off. She pulled the thin straps off her shoulders and the whole combination slid down her body, landing in a pile on the floor. I liked what I saw underneath. Smooth, pale skin, large boobs, a soft, round belly, and thick thighs.

I kept my clothes on as I approached her. There are two possible reasons for my doing this. Some women – and I stress the word "some" – like the feeling of vulnerability that comes from being naked in front of a fully-clothed man. In this case, though, I judged that Julie wanted me to start by focusing on her, without her feeling she had to reciprocate. I spent a long time kissing her. The tip of my tongue played against hers. Placing my hand at the back of her head, I pushed my tongue deeply into her mouth. She groaned with pleasure. I got the feeling it had been a long time since she'd been kissed with such passion. My instinct told me she was already wet and wouldn't have complained if I'd fucked her. But I took my time. I wanted William to catch her not only having sex but enjoying the best fuck of her life. I moved my right hand down to cup her left breast. Taking her nipple between finger and thumb, I twisted it gently. She didn't react, so I figured there wasn't any masochism in her sexual profile. This neither pleased nor concerned me. It was intelligence I could use to ensure a successful operation. Using my strong leg muscles, I lowered myself to the floor slowly, kissing her breasts and belly on the way. When I was in a crouch – a bull doesn't *kneel* before anyone – I kissed her mound. She parted her legs to give me access. Spreading her pussy lips with my fingers, I kissed and licked her clit. I didn't spend long on this and soon stood up so I could kiss her again. I put my left arm around her shoulders and my right at the fold where her buttocks met her thighs. With a swift bend of my legs, I took her in my arms and carried her to the bed. She wasn't petite, but I managed this with no problem. I've never met a woman who didn't love this. There's something about knowing a man is strong enough to pick her up that excites every one of them. I laid her on the bed. Raising her head, she watched as I stripped off. Appreciative noises emerged from the back of her throat as I revealed my broad chest and powerful arms. I stood in front of her, naked except for my white boxer shorts. Letting the anticipation build is as important when I disrobe as when a woman does it. When I lowered them, she said, 'Damn!' in a low voice. I could see why. My cock looked great. Most of that was down to nature, but she was partly responsible. Julie wasn't the most beautiful woman I'd ever met, but her body looked eminently fuckable. I was about to lie down on her right side, when she patted the bed on her left.

I understood why as she put her left hand around my cock. Many hot wives want the symbols of their marriage to be violated by their stud. One asked me to look through her wedding album and choose a photo to cum on. I picked the one where she was kissing her new husband, and left a nice jizz stripe across both their faces. Then there was one who put on her wedding dress and wanted me to fuck her roughly from behind. I managed to resist singing "Here Comes The Bride" during her orgasm. Another wife had me ejaculate over her wedding ring, and looked surprised that it didn't burst into flames.

Julie simply wanted to feel my cock against her wedding ring. While she was busy with that, I surreptitiously took a condom out of its packet so there'd be no pause in the action. I got on top of her. Older women are often aggressive lovers and, as soon as I entered her, she forcefully thrust back against my cock. This ruled out any chance of taking it slowly. I had no choice but to match her speed.

I still had her husband in the back of my mind. He wanted to catch us having sex. If we kept going like this, he'd find us lying together in a postcoital glow.

She had no such worries. Closing her eyes, she moaned loudly. That's when we heard the front door open. Maybe the timing was right, after all. William could open the door at the moment I made his wife cum – an ideal picture for any cuckold. But looking down, I saw her expression had changed. She was no longer lost in ecstasy. Her eyes were hard and cold as she said, 'I can't wait to see his face when he finds you here.'

Her choice of words worried me immediately. 'What?' I demanded.

'He doesn't know anything about this.'

I stopped thrusting and looked at her, open-mouthed. She continued, 'For a year, now, he's been fucking his executive assistant. It's payback time.'

She tried to wrap her legs around my lower back to stop me from moving, but I was too quick for her and stood up. When William came into the room, I wasn't inside his wife, which was something, I suppose. I was standing naked by his bed with a condom on my cock, so I couldn't claim I was there to read the gas meter.

I hoped we'd all be mature about it. I would say, 'I do apologize, sir. There seems to have been a terrible mistake. I was under the impression you knew about this and wanted it to happen.'

He would reply, 'That's perfectly all right, my dear fellow. It could have happened to anyone. Don't give it another thought.'

And she would take the opportunity to say, 'Darling, the fact that I've done this should tell you that we have a number of problems in our marriage. Maybe we should sit down and talk about them.'

In reality, I didn't have time to say a word, because he lunged at me, screaming, 'You bastard, I'll fucking kill you!' It was a good thing he tripped as his foot hit the bed leg and he fell against the wall. I grabbed my clothes and ran across the bed, hurdling Julie *en route*. I put my trousers on as I galloped down the stairs. I didn't think that was possible, either, but it's amazing what you can do when you have to. I slowed down when I realized William wasn't chasing me. He and Julie were working through their issues.

'This would never have happened if you weren't such a cheating asshole!'

'I wouldn't have cheated if you'd been a better wife!'

'I might have been a better wife if ....'

I didn't think there was anything I could usefully add to their discussion, so I let myself out the front door and got into my car. Driving home, I promised myself I'd never get involved with a couple again until I'd met *both* of them and knew they *both* wanted this to happen.

On Saturday evening, I drive to Ophelia's for my meeting with Jenna *and* Andy. I find a table where I can see the door. I've brought a book with me, so the evening isn't a complete waste of time if this turns out to be a no-show.

I order a sparkling water. I never drink alcohol at a first meeting. I have to stay sharp, picking up on all the little clues in the couple's behavior. The need to look after my body rules out calorie-laden drinks like Coke and orange juice.

Guys, you remember what it was like when you were first trying to impress the love of your life. You ate salad and went to the gym so you'd have a great body for the first time she saw you naked. Well, that's my permanent state. I go to bed with a woman for the first time at least once a month. It's one thing I envy about a man in a long-term relationship. He has the freedom to kick back with a hamburger and large fries. He can even top it off with an ice cream sundae if he so wishes. His wife or girlfriend might give his belly a censorious pat from time to time, but she still loves him and might even let him fuck her occasionally. I don't have this luxury. My body has to be ready to make a first impression every day of the year.

The door opens. Jenna and Andy come in. I know it's them, because Jenna matches Andy's description of her. This isn't always the case. Sometimes guys exaggerate the attractiveness of their partners. A man once told me, 'Imagine Angelina Jolie crossed with Megan Fox.' But when I met her, I thought, *Well, she has brown hair. Apart from that* …. Conversely, many a man has been with his partner so long he's stopped noticing how attractive she is. One guy even said, 'I should warn you, she's no beauty queen.' But when I met them, I found a girl with a lovely face and a nice, compact figure. I could imagine her doing well at a local pageant.

I see from Andy's eyes that he's nervous about meeting me, but he puts on a brave face and strides forward with his hand outstretched. 'You must be Daniel,' he says, speaking extra loudly to disguise the quaver in his voice.

'I am indeed,' I say, my own voice a model of quiet calm.

I turn to Jenna, who's not sure how to approach me. We don't know each other, and yet, we both know why we're there, so there's an automatic frisson between us. She's asking herself if we should kiss on the cheek, kiss on the lips …. I take a step toward her and shake her hand. At the first meeting, I like to treat both the man and the woman in the same way, reinforcing the idea that we're all fundamentally equal, even if we play unequal roles later in the game. 'Nice to meet you, Daniel,' she says. 'Are you always Daniel or can we call you Dan?' I give a little shrug, telling her she can call me whatever she likes. 'Are we late?' she asks, but carries on before I can answer. 'I was worried we wouldn't get here on time. It's been quite a day. My best friend from school's getting married in a couple of weeks. So, I need a dress that's nice, but not as nice as hers. We must have tried on twenty of the bloody things. But I didn't find one that spoke to me. You know what I mean?'

I nod. 'I always stress out when I'm buying a new dress.'

She has a soft, musical laugh. 'We met another friend for lunch.' It's good that she's sharing all this with me. But their life sounds so full I'm not sure there's room for me. 'We kept chatting until it was time to come and meet you.' She blushes. 'We couldn't tell Leo *who* we were meeting this evening, so we said you were an old work colleague. But of course, he was all, "Hey, I'll come too!" Fortunately, his girlfriend called, and he had to go round to her place. Could have been a bit awkward otherwise.'

As she talks, she looks me up and down with a little smile. She likes the way I'm put together. I'm immediately attracted to her. I would call her hair copper shimmer rather than strawberry blonde, but it's beautiful, whatever it is. Her eyes are bright blue and sparkling with excitement. She has a stripe of freckles across the top of her cheeks and the bridge of her nose. But I'm most struck by her huge smile, which makes her look friendly and a lot of fun. A nitpicker might say her teeth were slightly crooked, but so what? I don't find perfection interesting. If you look at a perfectly drawn triangle or circle, you might admire the geometry, but you don't appreciate it as art. For me, the most beautiful parts of a face are often the imperfections and asymmetry. She's dressed in black boots, jeans, and a lumberjack shirt with red and black checks. It's an outfit that could look manly, but no one seeing Jenna's well-rounded ass or ample chest would be in any doubt that she was all woman. I like that she's confident enough to know she doesn't need to wear see-through or low-cut clothes. She rises above such clichés.

I automatically scan her for signs about what she might like in bed. She looks like a generous lover – the type who would let a man cum in her mouth and go to sleep without expecting anything else. I make a mental note to rein her in if she tries to focus on me too much. There's also an unrestrained bubbliness about her that suggests she lets herself go when she cums. I have a feeling that, if *I* give her an orgasm, she'll scream loud enough to wake the whole street and her body will buck so hard, she'll break the bed. I very much want that to happen.

I guess she looks in the mirror once a week and says, 'I must lose weight.' But on a Saturday night, she and Andy go out with their friends and she enjoys a few drinks and a pizza. That's fine by me. I don't want to cut myself on her while we're fucking.

They sit down. Jenna orders a large glass of white wine for herself and a beer for Andy. Turning to me, she says, 'Anyway, how are *you*?'

'It's been a pretty boring day compared to yours. I had to work this morning.'

'What do you do?'

'I'm a fitness trainer.'

People are often surprised that I chose this line of work. Initially, I went into it as a way of paying my bills after I graduated. But the job sucked me in. I was told if I stayed six months, I could train other trainers. I liked the sound of this, so I stuck around. Then my boss told me that, after a year, I could design courses for other trainers to follow. This sounded interesting. I've been in the same job for eleven years now. I do think I'm not making the best use of an expensive education. I went to a good university, where I read psychology and sociology. My tutor advised me to train as a clinical psychologist. That would have been fascinating, and I might still go into it one day. But it wouldn't have been a good job for a bull. There's this damn code of ethics that stops psychologists from seducing their patients. Fitness trainers have no such code regarding our clients. Well, officially we do, but a lot of us take a flexible approach to it. A female client likes to talk as she's pounding out the miles on the treadmill. The trainer becomes her confidant. Many a woman has told me I'm the only man who listens to her. She appreciates the attention she gets from a good-looking guy, and a bond forms. I don't want you thinking there's anything exploitative in what I do. You might think bulls have no morals, and I don't claim to have many, but one rule I follow without deviation is that of never fucking anyone who's vulnerable. If a woman says her husband mistreats or neglects her, I gently suggest she should see a counselor. She might say she needs to feel loved one more time, but casual sex isn't the answer. She wants a man to lift her out of her marriage and take her to a better place. This is not what's on offer from me.

There are times when I'm talking with a client and she'll shyly admit that she and her husband have always had this fantasy .... After that, it goes the same way as any other encounter. I don't see why anything should change because we happened to meet at my place of work.

It's rarer, but I've also had encounters initiated by male clients. The men I see at work tend to come in two shapes and sizes. There are the guys who have been skinny all their lives and think half an hour of light weights will turn them into Joe Manganiello. Then there are the fat blokes whose doctors have told them to lose weight or die. One of them looks at me and makes a comment like, 'You're in good shape, man,' before adding, 'My wife would like you.'

That could be as far as it goes. This is a good time to say that the majority of potential encounters turn out to be dead ends. I've worked out that I end up having sex with one in ten of all the women I hear about who might be interested. That's a pretty good hit rate.

If it does go further, my client will be checking his phone when he "accidentally" shows me the photo of his wife that he's got set as wallpaper. In a voice that's a little too casual, he asks, 'What do you reckon to her, then?'

'Fine looking woman,' I always reply.

He's not sure if I'm just being polite. With a light laugh to show this is all a bit of fun, he asks, 'So, if you met her in a bar, do you think you'd be interested?'

I say, 'I would buy her a drink. We'd dance. If she agreed to come home with me, I'd think I was the luckiest man in the world.'

Here's another point where it could end. I've given him a pleasant little fantasy, which he may or may not share with his wife. Alternatively, I might find that, during our sessions, the conversation always gets back to the subject of her. He talks about how great she looked at the party on Saturday night and says, 'You should have been there.' Or his phone has a new picture of her on the beach in a bikini. 'What would you say if you ran into her wearing that?'

Then he might decide to take the plunge. Still using that don't-give-a-damn-one-way-or-another voice, he mentions at the end of an evening session, 'I'm meeting my wife for a drink afterwards. You know … if you'd like to come along … I'm sure she'd love to meet you.'

I'm not going to say no, am I? After I've showered, I put on the smart shirt I keep in my locker for times like this and we head out together. She might be surprised. Expecting a quiet drink with her husband, she's suddenly confronted with a hot black guy. Other times, she's there in a sexy outfit with perfect hair and make-up. She looks up slyly from her drink as we walk in and I know they've cooked this up together. Either way, I turn on the charm and see where the evening takes us.

Another advantage of my job is that it makes it easier for me to look after myself. The sixty-year-old trainers who were bodybuilders back in the day have large bellies now they've dialed down the heavy lifting, and the clients accept that as a natural progression. We younger guys have to look like we knock off a triathlon before breakfast. This is good for my life as a bull. There are couples who fantasize about the woman going with a fat, ugly guy. It's the ultimate insult to the husband: *Even this troll is preferable to you, darling.* But, they're few and far between. Most cuckold fantasies revolve around a stud who's fit in both senses of the word. I might find it hard to keep that up if I spent all day sitting in a room, talking to the patients in my clinical psychology practice.

A trainer's pay isn't great, but I make a lot in tips. A businessman who credits me with staving off his third heart attack will often finish our session by slipping me an envelope with a couple of twenties in it. I do need this money. The bull lifestyle is not cheap. When I started down this road, I realized I'd need my own flat. I couldn't imagine seducing anyone with the words, 'Come back to my place, but we have to be quiet or we'll wake my mum.' Apartments in London are famously expensive, but I didn't need a big place. One bedroom would be enough: if a couple stays over with me, the cuckold accepts that his place is on the couch. I found it is possible to get a bargain if you're prepared to go to a more down-market part of town. I thought this might put women off, but I discovered that, for a lot of them, the opposite is true. A respectable woman who lives in a big house with her company director husband often wants to rough it a little when she's with her stud. So long as she's not in danger, she likes the idea of seeing what she imagines to be life on the mean streets.

However, once we get *into* my place, she wants to see that things are a bit plushier. I've known women who fantasize about being thrown down and fucked in the mud or having sex with a tramp in a dumpster, but I suspect these fantasies aren't often made real. Generally, when people take their clothes off, they want to do it somewhere hygienic. So, I spend a lot of time cleaning my apartment, making sure every inch of it is prepared for a naked woman.

When fitting out my place, the first requirement was a double bed. I couldn't skimp on this. The bed would see a lot of action, so needed to be sturdy, but also luxurious – the type of bed on which any woman would be glad to stretch out. The other biggest expense was the bathroom. I needed a bath big enough for two, with the taps in the middle, and also a shower. Some women like going home with a black man's semen on their tits. Others don't. So, I needed a quick and easy way for them to clean up before returning to their nice, respectable world.

The other thing I had to spend money on was a car. 'Let's go back my place – the Fiat Panda's right outside,' is also not a good line for a bull. I got lucky there. A friend of mine had an old Jaguar. He'd discovered that driving around the gridlocked streets of London isn't much fun and the car had sat in his garage for the last three years. He was willing to sell at a reduced price. When I took my father round to look at it, he pronounced that, with a bit of work, it would run nicely. I bought it and spent a couple of bonding weekends with my dad. In theory, he was teaching me car maintenance. Really, I watched admiringly as he worked his magic. By the end of the second weekend, I had a shiny, deep red car that always gets an appreciative gasp from people seeing it for the first time. When I'm driving a couple back to my place, the husband can avoid uncomfortable silences by asking how many miles to the gallon I get.

All this meant I had to borrow money from my parents, which I duly paid back. I also took out a bank loan, which I'm still paying off. But I had everything I needed to be a stud: a hot car and a swish apartment. I was ready to begin.

'How do you know Paula?' I ask Jenna.

Her eyes light up. 'She's one of my best friends. She took me under her wing when I started my first job.'

'What did she say about me?'

Jenna blushes again. It makes her look so shy and sweet that I want to hug her. 'I don't want to stroke your ego too much.'

'I'm used to a bit of stroking,' I reply.

Waggling her eyebrows, she says, 'I bet you are. Anyway, a few weeks ago, a bunch of us were in the City Bar and Grill – do you know it?' I shake my head. 'Andy wasn't there. It was a girls' night out. It got to be midnight. There was no sign of the place closing, so we ordered a couple more bottles of wine. Conversation turned to sex. We went round the table asking, "What's the best you've ever had?" Jackie said it was with this German guy she met when she was working in Hamburg. I – obviously – said Andy's the best.' She casts an affectionate sideways look at her boyfriend. 'I wasn't lying.' Now it's his turn to blush. 'But when it got to Paula's turn, she ….' Jenna bites her lip and looks at me mischievously. 'Let's say, she told us some interesting things.' Jenna's right in that my ego's healthy enough without any stroking, but it would be nice to hear what Paula says about me. 'I got home at two in the morning and slipped into bed next to Andy,' says Jenna. 'He was half-awake and half-erect. That soon changed when he realized I was naked. He asked me how my night had been and I said, "Paula told us a story about her friend, Daniel. Apparently, he's this tasty black guy who comes round to her place and fucks her while Ray watches. She says the sex is Absolutely. Mind. Blowing." Andy put his hand between my legs and felt how wet I was. He asked how that made me feel. I said, "Strangely excited and … a little bit jealous." I don't know how much Andy told you on the phone, but we've always loved fantasizing about me with other guys. So ….' She gives me a look that's almost embarrassed. 'I hope you don't mind, Daniel, but we switched the light off and pretended Andy was you. I didn't know what you looked like, so I had to imagine. But … I wasn't too far off the mark.'

'So, really, you've already had sex with me. But you used Andy's body to do it.'

'Mm,' she says, as if she's not sure about that. 'It was hot sex, anyway. I didn't want to talk afterwards. I was drunk and we were both tired, so we went to sleep. The next day, I asked Andy, "How would you feel if we gave Daniel a call?" And after we'd finished having sex again, he said, "It can't hurt to meet him for a drink." I reached into my bag and took out a piece of paper. "Paula happened to give me Daniel's number," I said. And after we'd finished having sex again, I said, "Why don't you give him a call?" And after we'd ....'

'I'm glad you did,' I say.

'How long have you ... been ...?'

'A bull?' I prompt.

She laughs. 'I didn't know that was the word.'

'Some people prefer "stud." I answer to both.'

'I like the idea of being with a *bull*. Sounds more exciting than a man. So, how long have you been ... bulling?'

'Seven years now.'

She leans toward me as if she's conducting an interview. 'A deliberate career choice or did you fall into it?'

I didn't think I was going to be a bull – at least, not after a certain age. Believe it or not, there was a time when I liked the idea of being married. I was popular with the girls at school and university. I had plenty of opportunities to hone my sexual technique, but shied away from long-term relationships. Nevertheless, I assumed I was sowing wild oats in my youth and would look for something serious before too long. I did look. I was 21 when I shyly asked the people in my circle if they knew anyone who could be my girlfriend. As you can imagine, I already had quite a reputation and my request caused surprise and amusement. One friend even asked if I had to settle down because I was pregnant. But another said he knew a girl I might like. He set me up with an Irish girl called Fiona. She and I met at a nice Italian restaurant one Friday evening. She wasn't exactly beautiful, but she was certainly pretty. She had shoulder length brown hair and blue eyes. We clicked immediately. First dates can be tricky as you try to make polite conversation: 'The weather was disappointing today. The situation in the Middle East continues to be troubling, does it not?'

Fiona and I didn't have that. I happened to mention that I was excited because one of my friends had got us tickets to see the Rolling Stones. Fiona grimaced and said, 'Oh, I can't stand them.' You might think this would have been a negative – something we didn't have in common. But I liked her for it. Often on a first date, people agree to everything. The woman says, 'On Saturday afternoons, I like to fill my bath with custard and splash around in it.' And the man replies, 'No kidding! That's what I do, as well!'

I appreciated Fiona's honesty and we went straight to the teasing banter of people who'd been friends for years. There was no nastiness as we gently took the piss out of each other. Halfway through the evening, I was sure I'd made a friend, but I didn't think it was going to be more than that. We laughed a lot and were having a good time, but I couldn't detect any flirting going on. I liked her soft Irish accent, but wouldn't have called it sexy. When we finished dinner, we decided to go for a drink. Leaving the restaurant, she stumbled, and I put my arm around her shoulder to steady her. She immediately responded by putting her arm around my waist. She did this so quickly I wasn't sure if she'd genuinely stumbled or if it had been a ploy. My suspicions increased as she found fault with every pub and bar we tried. Music too loud. Lights too bright. Clientele too pretentious. After she'd rejected the fifth place, she said, 'You know, we could always have a drink back at my place. It's only twenty minutes on the train.'

When we arrived at her flat, we sat on her couch, sipping her wine. The conversation that had flowed so freely dried up. We knew we were there to have sex, and neither of us wanted to speak in case we said something stupid and broke the spell. After fifteen awkward minutes, I knew I had to make a move. I drained my glass, and put it on the table. Placing my hands on her shoulders, I drew her toward me and kissed her. Her lips moved against mine and she put her hand behind my head to pull me closer. She was wearing a blue shirt with silver poppers on it. I liked this: no buttons to fiddle with. Kissing her neck, I pushed her shirt away from her left shoulder. I moved my lips down until they reached her left breast. She was wearing a simple white bra. Its job was to support rather than to arouse. This is exactly what did arouse me. It meant she hadn't come out that night to get laid. She'd been on a fact-find to see what I was like. Such was my allure that she'd found herself in this unexpected position.

She reached behind her back to undo the fastening and the bra fell into her lap. Smiling proudly, she pushed her chest toward me. I could see why she was proud. She had 38d breasts. That's my preferred upper limit for breast size. I know a lot of guys like huge boobs. But I always think if they're too big, it's like the woman has a couple of balloons stuffed down her shirt. They become comical rather than sexy. Fiona's *were* sexy, and I could feel my cock pressing against the front of my trousers.

Standing up, she led me into the bedroom. I laid her gently on the bed. She put her hands behind her head. She had stubble and a few longer rogue hairs in each armpit. It wasn't a lifestyle choice: she just hadn't bothered to shave. This turned me on, as well. It was further evidence that she hadn't planned to have sex. I kissed my way down her body until I reached her panties. They were in the same simple white material as her bra. I pulled them down. Her pussy lips were hidden behind a puff of brown pubes. I used my thumbs to open her up gently. Dipping my head down, I licked along her inner lips. She gasped, more with surprise than pleasure. She told me later that her last boyfriend hadn't been a big fan of cunnilingus, despite his enthusiasm for fellatio. It had taken weeks to encourage him even to give her cunt a fleeting kiss. So, it was a pleasant shock when she felt my tongue on her during our first time.

Even in those days, I had confidence in my virility. But, as a precaution, I took Fiona halfway to orgasm with my tongue. Sliding a condom over my cock, I penetrated her. It was a ham-fisted maneuver by the standards I have for myself now, but slicker than the panicked fumbling of most 21-year-olds. Looking into her eyes, I saw trust. She was confident that I knew what I was doing and would give her a good time. I didn't disappoint her. I fucked her slowly, watching her face all the time. It wasn't long before her eyes rolled back in her head and she came with a cry of, 'Fuck, yeah!' She took a moment to let the feeling sink in before looking up with a grin. 'Okay, Daniel, show me what you've got!' She didn't grip the bed, but her face showed she was bracing herself. After a green light like that, I didn't hold back. I rammed myself into her as hard and as fast as I could. She looked excited but scared, like she was jumping out of a plane for the first time. It was clear she'd never experienced anything like this. She was getting close to a second orgasm. These days, I'd slow down and let it happen. Back then, I kept going until I ejaculated. Without taking even a second to appreciate it, I went down and licked her pussy until she came again.

My first time with Fiona was like a great rock band's debut album. It showed plenty of raw talent, but lacked the polish and professionalism of later work. Nevertheless, she was more than happy. Laying her head on my chest, she looked up at me with shining eyes and said, 'I wouldn't mind doing that again some time.'

'I'll check my diary,' I said, smiling.

She fell asleep soon after that. At first, I thought it was a post-coital doze, but when her breathing deepened, I realized she was gone for the night. I've never been one to sneak out on a woman without telling her, so I resigned myself to sleeping there too. It wasn't a comfortable night. With Fiona's head on my chest, I couldn't move. I was painfully aware that I hadn't brushed my teeth. I could feel acid from the wine burning holes in the enamel. Her body was pressed into mine, with her boobs warm and soft against my side. I soon had an erection again, but there was nothing I could do with it. I didn't want to wake her, and I wasn't going to do anything to her while she was asleep. It felt wrong to pleasure myself while I was in bed with a naked woman. All I could do was lie there and think about what might happen when she woke up. I didn't think I'd slept at all, but I was suddenly aware of the sun streaming in under her curtains.

She blinked as the light hit her face and she rolled off me. I took the opportunity to slip out of bed and tiptoe to her bathroom. I peed, washed my face, and stole a bit of her toothpaste so my breath would be minty fresh when she woke up. I lay on the bed next to her, but didn't get under the blankets. She was lying on her back. The blankets had slid down to expose her breasts. I looked at them and soon my cock was hard again. She woke up and gave the little start of someone who'd forgotten she had company in her bed. She relaxed immediately as she remembered the night before. Smiling contentedly, she said, 'Good morning.' Her eyes travelled down my body and her grin broadened when she saw my cock. 'And good morning to you, sir.' Returning her gaze to my face, she asked, 'Why don't you get properly attired?' I rolled a condom over my cock. Putting my hand between her legs, I felt that she was wet enough. There was no need for foreplay, so I got on top of her. She grabbed the base of my cock and fed it into her cunt – not something anyone would have to do for me these days. Closing her eyes, she moaned as I moved inside her. I could tell she was enjoying it, but maybe she wasn't awake enough to feel everything. It was one time when I came before the woman did. If that happened now, I'd go into a back room with a gun and take the honorable course. Even back then, I was disappointed in myself and sought to make amends. Rolling myself into a ball between her legs, I licked her clit vigorously until her body tensed and she came with a little high-pitched scream.

Afterwards, I put my arms around her. I was aware of two things. The first was that I liked this girl and wanted to spend more time with her. The second was that I *really* liked having sex with her, and wanted to do it hundreds of times. An obvious way of achieving both objectives presented itself. 'So, Fiona,' I began, 'if people point at you and ask me, "Who's that lovely girl over there?" is it okay if I reply, "She's my girlfriend"?'

She was silent for a while. I could tell she was thinking it through. Fucking me was one thing. Dating was another. There have never been many black people in Ireland, and she was wondering how her family and friends would react to me.

Her eyes hardened into a look that said, *Sorry if you don't approve, mother, but I'm going to do this.* 'Yes, I'm your girlfriend,' she said, firmly. There was only one possible response to this. I fucked her again. Afterwards, we decided that, as we were now a couple, we should do something couply, so we went out for breakfast. Conversation didn't flow as well as it had the night before. She lapsed into silences and I could tell she was thinking about how – or if – she should tell her family about me. When we got back to her place, we fucked again, which eased the tension nicely.

I never knew how much she did tell her family about me. I figured that wasn't my business. There was a sea between us and them, so it's not like they were going to come and visit any time soon. I heard her on the phone, talking about Danny or possibly Dani. So maybe, as far as they were concerned, I was her friend of indeterminate sex and color.

While we're on the subject, I'm often asked if there's any racism in interracial cuckoldry. There *is* racial stereotyping. The fantasy is that *all* black guys are tall and well-muscled, have huge cocks, fuck all night, and make a woman cum ten times. I know I do nothing to disprove this. But the fact is, some black guys are skinny, while others are fat. I have black friends who are shy around girls and don't have much luck with them. In the gym showers, I see that not all black men are prodigiously well-endowed.

But if racism is defined as prejudice *against* people of a certain race, I would say interracial cuckoldry is the opposite: it's prejudice *in favor* of black men. If there's a victim here, it's the white guy who suffers from the belief that he's incapable of satisfying his woman. Again, I know this to be an unfair generalization. I've met women who have turned down my advances and told me they're happy with the sex they get from their white husbands. Some of them said that out of loyalty, but not all. I've got a good eye for spotting if a woman is frustrated or not, and a lot of these women looked satisfied. They'd have been *more* satisfied if they'd taken advantage of my offer, but that's their choice.

The first three months with Fiona were great. Taking the train to see her was always exciting. She would send text messages telling me what she was wearing and what she was going to do to me as soon as I got in the door. It's the only time I've enjoyed a train delay. If we stopped for ten minutes outside the station with no explanation, it felt like a delicious tease. The waiting would make the moment of seeing her even sweeter.

When I arrived at her place, I barely made it inside before she was reaching into my pants. I spent many happy minutes with my butt pressed against her front door while she knelt in front of me, sucking my cock. Her mouth was wonderfully warm and soft, but I never let it carry on too long. She told me it was okay if I wanted to cum in her mouth, but that's never been my thing. I soon moved her head away and crouched down beside her. I kissed her tenderly, never minding the taste of my cock on her lips. Why should I feel any revulsion at that? I take it as a compliment when a woman sucks my cock, and the taste only reminds me of the privilege I've enjoyed. Pushing her onto the floor, I lay on top of her and kissed her again. The first couple of times we fucked in her little hallway, she was wearing jeans, and there was clumsy maneuvering in a tight space as we got them off her. She soon started answering the door in a skirt. It wasn't long afterwards that she abandoned all pretense of modesty and slipped her panties off before I arrived. Her excitement at seeing me again and sucking my cock meant she was always ready for me to get inside her. This wasn't a time for niceties. This was an urgent, *I've missed you so much* fuck. I always screwed her hard and fast.

I never failed to bring her to orgasm in our hallway fucks. *I* didn't cum if I wanted to save myself for later. But when I did cum, it wasn't inside her, as we didn't take the time to put on a condom. (I know. We were young.) She pulled up whatever top she was wearing and let me shoot my load over her belly.

After we'd finished, we got on with being a couple. We went out a lot. She had a nice group of friends, who accepted me as one of their own. We spent many pleasant evenings in bars and restaurants. Otherwise, the two of us sat and chatted over a coffee or a glass of wine. But there was always an undercurrent of sex. We'd fucked on the day we met, so it was in our relationship from the beginning. Whatever we did in the evening, we knew we'd go back to her place afterwards and have sex. If I stayed over at hers, we fucked before we went to sleep, and, when we woke up, we did it again. Not a day went by when we didn't have sex at least twice. Often, it was four or five times. One evening, she looked at me in post-orgasmic joy and said, 'I am a nymphomaniac!' Obviously, she wasn't, in the strict sense. But we throw the word around to describe any highly-sexed woman. I was happy to be with a woman who loved sex as much as I did.

We tried several variations. I spanked her a few times, but she always liked the *idea* of it more than the actual feeling. I tied her up once, but we both agreed it was a bit silly. I never did anything to her that she would try to stop, so what was the point in her being restrained? She had no interest in anal sex, which *did* disappoint me, I must admit. I'd enjoyed experimenting with a couple of the girls at university.

I still appreciate the heat and tightness of a well-oiled asshole. It's different from the vagina. There's also the psychological thrill when a woman's actions tell me, *I'm prepared to perform this illicit act with you. There are porn stars who won't do this, but I'm going to do it with you because you turn me on so much.*

Fiona's real passion – something I'd never encountered before – was for name-calling. I don't mean she wanted me to say her name. A month into our relationship, we were in bed. I was kissing her breast when she remarked reflectively, 'The word "whore" keeps going round my head.'

I wasn't sure what she meant, so I said what I hoped was a joke. 'You want me to pay every time I fuck you?'

She laughed. 'The way we go at it, you'd be broke inside a week.

I feel like a whore, lying here, naked, letting a man do everything he wants to me.'

Well, not everything. But I didn't say that. 'Does it bother you?'

She took my hand and placed it between her legs. 'Feel how much it bothers me,' she said. Two of my fingers slipped easily into her wet pussy. 'How do you feel being in bed with a whore?' I followed her lead and put her hand on my hard cock. 'What else am I?' she asked.

I had to be careful. One wrong word could get me kicked out of bed. It could even end the relationship. She might be turned on if I called her a slut, but outraged if I used the word "bitch." 'You're … a tart,' I told her. I figured "tart" was less extreme than "whore," so I'd be safe here.

She enthusiastically agreed. 'I'm your dirty little tart,' she said. 'What else?'

I decided to risk it. 'You're a slut.'

It worked. 'I'm a white slut for your big, black cock.'

It turned out she was open to all the bad names I could think of. It became a regular part of our sex play. She moaned with excitement as I told her, 'You're my whore, Fiona. A cock-happy little bitch who lives to be fucked.'

One time, she told me, 'I'm a cheap *Irish* whore for you.' This was a surprise. Fiona had always been proud of her nationality. After we'd both cum, I asked her about this. She replied that it made it personal. Anyone could be a whore. But fewer had the right to call themselves Irish whores. It was like when she described herself as "a big-titted whore." She had nothing against her big tits. Apart from the occasional twinge of backache, she liked them. But the insult was personal to her if it highlighted one of her features.

These were happy times. I had a girlfriend I liked. We had a good time together. We had great sex. We were clearly meant for each other and even had a few conversations about getting married.

But things started to change. I arrived at her place, and she was wearing her jeans again. She gave me a kiss, rather than sucking my cock. I made a move to get her onto the hall floor, but she pushed me away with a teasing smile, saying, 'Later, Danny. The film starts in twenty minutes, and I want to get snacks.' Missing the trailers and foregoing popcorn was a small price to pay for a quickie on the floor. It struck me that a true nymphomaniac would realize that. At least that time, we had sex when we came back from the cinema. So, I went to sleep happy enough. But there was the time when we got into bed and she told me, 'I'm not feeling sexy tonight.'

In my most seductive voice, I said, 'It's my job to get you in the mood, then.'

She shook her head. 'Tomorrow.'

She rolled over and went to sleep. I lay next to her, feeling that all was not right with the world. I was in bed with my girlfriend. We were both naked, but no sex was happening. I finally got my hormones to calm down enough so I could sleep. When I woke up, she was not beside me, naked and keen to make amends. She was already dressed and cooking breakfast.

As we saw each other more and more, we fucked each other less and less. She suggested I keep a set of my gym clothes at her place. It would save me having to rush back to my folks' house before going to work.

Without my realizing it, we were sort of living together. I had no objection to this idea. Naively, I thought it would lead to increased sex. People talk about sex and intimacy as if they're the same. But in fact, they're diametrically opposed. When Fiona and I first got together, nudity meant sex. She showed me her body to excite me, so I'd fuck her. As we spent more time sharing the same space, I discovered she was frequently naked for reasons that had nothing to do with sex. Maybe you know what it's like. Your wife or girlfriend's getting changed, when she turns to you, scratches under her tit and says, 'We're out of toilet cleaner. We must remember to pick some up next time we're near the shops.' Can anyone tell me what's supposed to be sexy about that? Fiona also enjoyed taking long, hot baths. Plenty of erotic potential there. However, she liked me to sit on the edge of the bath and listen while she talked about her day. She lay there with beads of sweat running down her breasts, so visually it was great. But she'd say, 'I did at least three quarters of the work on that project, but Alan acts like it was all him. I should have spoken up in the meeting and told them what I'd done, but I just sat there.' Not my idea of pillow talk.

Living together is not about sex every night. It's about eating the food you like *sometimes* and going to bed when you want *if you're lucky*. It's also about watching TV shows you don't want to see. Fiona was a smart girl but, nonetheless, she loved soap operas. She was proud of having watched certain series from the start without missing an episode. I never pretended to like these programs, but she insisted I watch them with her and even enjoyed my squirming as I sat there, bored out of my mind. There were a hundred things I would rather have done with my time. But Fiona chose her soaps even over sex. Again, not what you'd expect from a self-proclaimed nymphomaniac.

One Sunday morning, I had the startling realization that I hadn't had sex in six weeks – despite the fact that I was essentially living with my girlfriend. This seemed fundamentally wrong to me – although I've since spoken to a lot of husbands and live-in boyfriends who say it's normal.

I asked Fiona about it and she said our relationship had evolved to a point where sex was no longer necessary. It was enough for us to cuddle. She also made the odd comment, 'If there's ice cream in the freezer, you know you can eat it tomorrow, or the next day, or whenever you want. So why would you eat it today?' All I can say is, sex was still of vital importance to me and, if I've got ice cream in my freezer, I want to eat it *today*, and have *more* – preferably of a different flavor – tomorrow. (In reality, my need to keep in shape means I hardly ever eat ice cream – but she started the analogy, not me.)

We stayed together for eight months before quietly deciding to call it a day. We were both sad, but neither of us was broken-hearted. We still had memories of how good it had once been. We went our separate ways, but stayed on good terms. We still occasionally hit each other up on Facebook. She's moved back to

Ireland, where she lives with her redhead husband – giving the lie to the old *Once you go black ...* cliché – and a couple of cute, freckly children. Life seems to have worked out okay for her, and I'm glad about that.

This wasn't when I gave up on the idea of having a girlfriend. I assumed that, if Fiona wasn't the one, someone else would be. Two weeks after we split up, I found myself sitting next to Jocelyn at a friend's dinner party. This might have been an accident, but I suspect my friend engineered it.

Jocelyn had smooth, black hair, captivating dark eyes, an upturned nose, and teeth that had been made to sparkle at great expense. I can't say we spent the whole evening talking. *I* talked and she spent the evening *listening*. At one point, she said, 'I don't talk much.' This should have been a warning. What it meant was, *People pay attention to me because of my looks, so I don't need to try.* At the end of the evening, she wrote her number on a serviette and said, 'Give me a ring.'

It would have been good for her soul if I'd never called her, but I'm as big a sucker for beauty as the next guy. I phoned her two days later and we went out to dinner. Again, she assumed it was my responsibility to entertain and charm her. She was doing her bit if she smiled and nodded occasionally. Her sense of entitlement was still more obvious when the bill arrived. She didn't even make a feint of reaching for her purse. It was only fitting that the man should pay for everything. Feminism was for other – less attractive – women. I was annoyed by this but, when she invited me back to her place, I agreed immediately.

In bed too, she expected me to do all the work, but I didn't mind this so much. Physically, she was a change from Fiona. Fiona came up to my shoulder and had a body that was nicely big and curvy. Jocelyn was barely five foot with a figure made up of straight lines. Her tits were small with unobtrusive nipples that were only slightly darker than the rest of her skin. Her legs and armpits were perfectly smooth and had all the signs of having been done professionally. Her vulva was so small and discreet that, at first, I couldn't find her vagina. I finally located it hidden behind one of the delicate folds of skin. I wasn't sure she could take a cock like mine. It turned out she could, so long as I went slowly. I learned valuable lessons about being sensitive to any signs of pain or discomfort.

Jocelyn never swore. You have to believe me when I say she reacted to missing a bus by saying, 'Oh, bother.' So, when we were having sex, she avoided nouns altogether. Her tits were "them," while her cunt was "it." She said, 'You can kiss them,' or, 'I don't mind you licking it.' She'd have blushed to say "screw" and spontaneously combusted if the word "fuck" had ever passed her lips. So, sex between us was always called "making love." She once paid me a muted compliment when she said, 'You're really quite good at making love.'

Believing it wasn't possible to *make* love unless you were *in* love, she decided we must love each other. She informed me of this after we'd fucked for the third time.

These days, I'm an expert at tailoring the sex to the person. Back then, I fell into the trap of thinking what worked on one would work on all. As I was kissing Jocelyn's neck one evening, I murmured in her ear, 'You are such a whore for me.'

It got a reaction, but not the one I wanted. This quiet and reserved woman turned on me with the speed and ferocity of a terrier. 'Is that what you think of me? I make love with you and that makes me a common streetwalker?'

Trying to backpedal, I made another classic mistake. 'Of course, I don't think that. It's just that Fiona—'

I didn't think Jocelyn could get any angrier, but her voice went up in both pitch and volume as she screamed, 'You're thinking about your ex? If you'd rather be with her, you know what you can do!'

I didn't so much apologize as prostrate myself at Jocelyn's feet and beg her forgiveness – not something I would do today. It worked. After twenty minutes of my groveling, she forgave me and lay back in her *take me* position. I fucked her, but with a melancholy for times past. I'd enjoyed the name-calling games I'd played with Fiona. It was sad to think I might never do anything like that again.

Like Fiona, Jocelyn was into things I couldn't stand. With Jocelyn, it was at the other end of the cultural scale. In every relationship, the question will be asked, 'What's your favorite film?' It's safe to say *Star Wars* or *The Lord of the Rings*. They're mainstream enough that you won't sound geeky. If you don't mind a bit of geek, *2001 A Space Odyssey* is a good bet. Other people say *When Harry Met Sally* to show they're romantic, but with a quirky side. Then there are the classic film buffs who go with *Citizen Kane* or *Vertigo*. All of these are acceptable answers. But when I asked Jocelyn this question, she cited a 1956 Greek film called *O Drakos*. I'm sorry, but it isn't possible for anyone's favorite film to have a name like *O Drakos*. Foreign cinema is like classical music: no one actually likes it, but they pretend in order to look intellectual. I found myself fidgeting as much through subtitled films as I ever had through soap operas.

Sex with Jocelyn didn't trail off the way it had with Fiona. She never rejected me. She always seemed to enjoy it in her demure way. She came with a gentle sigh rather than a full-throated scream, but a cum's a cum for all that, so I didn't mind. I had as much sex as I wanted, but on one note. No variation, and always in the good old fashioned missionary position. If I suggested she ride me or we try doggy style, she said, 'I like to feel you on top of me.' You've realized by now that I'm open when it comes to talking about sex. With Jocelyn, however, I was tongue-tied. When a girl's so reserved she can't bring herself to say "boobs" or "pussy," it's hard to tell her you want to cum over her tits or fuck her roughly from behind. She did once kiss the side of my cock, but I could see her psyching herself up for it like she was diving off the high board. She gave me one hand job in all the time I knew her. But she treated my semen like it was radioactive and made me wear a condom so she didn't get anything on her hand.

Sometimes when I asked her if she wanted to have sex, she'd make a comment like, 'I suppose so. You did buy me dinner.' If I took her out, paid for everything, and generally gave her what she was entitled to, she had sex with me. That was her side of the bargain.

One evening, I lay in the bath, thinking over my experiences with Jocelyn and Fiona. I enjoyed having sex with them. But I didn't like all the additional things I was expected to do in my role as boyfriend. I'm sure scientists would say two was not a big enough sample group on which to base a conclusion about all relationships. Nonetheless, I decided they were always best at the beginning, when everything was fresh and exciting. Afterwards, there was the inevitable descent into the dull and familiar. *Was it inevitable?* Was there any way of managing my sex life so this didn't happen? I thought about becoming a bastard. I could meet a woman, have sex with her, string her along until boredom set in, and dump her. But I didn't want to do that. I hope that's another point God will take into account when deciding which way to send me. It wasn't fair to make a woman believe I loved her and then leave her on her own. But, I reflected, what about the women who *wouldn't* be on their own after I left? In other words, what about the women who were already with someone? I could become one of those guys who have affairs with bored married women, making them feel attractive again after their husbands have lost interest. But this gave me another pang of conscience. It might reduce the hurt suffered by the women, but what about the men? How many husbands would be devastated if they knew their beloved wives had been sneaking around and having an affair? It wouldn't be right to do this to guys who had done me no harm.

I got out of the bath and onto my computer. My first search was crude, but surprisingly useful. I typed "cheating" into Google. I found definitions of the word and links to news stories about celebrities who'd been doing the dirty on their partners. One link asked the question, "What counts as cheating?" Clicking on it, I found a page that discussed flirting, sexting, and chatting online. It told readers forcefully they were *all* forms of cheating. At the end of the article, there was a paragraph that included words I hadn't seen used before in this context. There were women who didn't *cheat* on their husbands. Rather, they were *shared*. These women were called *hot wives*. Their husbands actively encouraged them to have sex with other men. These men were called *cuckolds*. Most importantly for me, the men who had sex with these hot wives were known as *bulls* or *studs*. Another word I saw was *zelophilia*. It was a word that sounded so strange I checked several sources to make sure it existed. I discovered it means finding erotic pleasure in one's own or another person's jealousy.

It was like when you see an advertisement for your ideal job. I sat up and read it through a couple of times, in case it was too good to be true. But, my initial understanding of the situation was correct. If I became one of these bulls or studs, I could meet different women all the time. I'd have the interest of getting to know a new person without the exhaustion of reaching the level of intimacy required of a boyfriend. There'd be all the bits I liked without the downsides. No tedious conversation every day. No watching programs and films I didn't like.

But how do you become a bull? I found my way to cuckold websites and posted ads. I got fed up with all the time wasters who came back to me. After a while, I realized that being a bull is like being a plumber. It's all about word-of-mouth. One person's satisfied with the service I offer, so she tells her friends. They tell their friends, and my reputation grows. Now my phone rings at least twice a week with a fresh enquiry from a hot wife or a nervous cuckold.

'Do you think you'll ever try again?' asks Jenna. 'Go down the road of a "normal" relationship again?'

I nod. 'Good question. At some point, I'll have to give this up. A bull over fifty is inevitably going to be called "daddy," and that's not my thing.'

'I'll stop myself in time,' says Jenna. Putting on an ecstatic voice, she moans, 'Oh, fuck me, da ... da ... damn, you're hot!'

I laugh and carry on, 'The day will come when my abs dissolve into a bag of fat, and all the crunches in the world won't get them back. That's when I have to admit traditional relationships come into their own. Someone who loves you will forgive a sagging body and gray pubic hairs.'

They exchange smiles. 'Andy has a couple of gray pubes,' she says. 'They make his cock look distinguished.'

'Or "old" as we say in English,' he adds.

He looks like he's about to say something else, but settles for taking a sip of his drink. 'He's too polite to point out that my body sags a bit more than when we first met,' says Jenna.

He kisses her on the cheek. 'It's still the sexiest body in the world.'

Jenna and Andy are a solid couple. They listen to each other, a sure sign of mutual respect. When Jenna speaks, Andy rests his cheek in his hand and listens, nodding occasionally. When Andy speaks, Jenna looks at him and occasionally interjects with an 'Mm' of agreement. They don't talk over, contradict, or ridicule each other.

In fact, these two are so much in love I think maybe I should butt out so they can go home and fuck each other. But I ask, 'How did you two get together?'

They exchange a *Do you want to take this?* look. By a secret means of communication, they agree Jenna should speak first. 'Have you ever met someone who was like your best friend from the first moment?'

I nod sadly, thinking about the first time I met Fiona.

'That's how it was with us,' Jenna continues. 'We met at a friend's party and could talk about anything immediately.'

'With me, it was knowing that I wanted to spend as much time with Jenna as possible,' says Andy. 'We tried being friends for a while after we met. But friends spend the day together, then say, "Let's do this again, next week, or the week after." That didn't work for us. I needed to see Jenna every day, so ....'

'So, becoming a couple was the only option,' says Jenna.

'We've been together five years. Engaged for the last six months. I wanted to get my career on track so I could reassure Jenna's dad we won't be looking for handouts.'

'It sounds like you're living the dream,' I say. 'So—?'

'Where do you fit in?' she asks.

'Exactly.'

She takes a deep breath, smiles at me sweetly and says, 'Fuck, cunt, cock.'

I raise my eyebrows. 'Yes, the weather *has* been quite cold for the time of year.'

She laughs. 'I want to make it clear we're all adults. We know why we're here, so let's not pussyfoot around. I'm a verbal person. Everyone I know has asked me if I ever stop talking. I'm not about to take a vow of silence because I'm having sex. So, don't be surprised if you hear the world's dirtiest commentator describing the action. And ... I want the guy to do the same.'

I turn to Andy. 'You don't like to talk? You're the man of action who lets his cock do the talking?'

He shakes his head. 'I get tongue-tied.'

'I've asked him to talk dirty to me so many times,' says Jenna.

'And all I can think of is, "I'm fucking you, Jenna .... I'm still fucking you, Jenna .... Can you feel me fucking you, Jenna?"'

'Which is fine,' she says. 'But I want a little more.'

I don't admit that I've been tongue-tied myself during sex: that was the old me. 'You want me to say I'm going to stick my big, black cock up your tight, white cunt and fuck you until you cum like a bitch?'

This elicits a quiet moan from both of them. Jenna says, 'I hope you won't mind if I say your balls are banging into my fat ass.'

I raise my eyebrows and take a quick look under the table. 'I wouldn't say your ass is fat.'

'Yes, you would. I've got the fattest ass you've ever seen.' Turning to Andy, she says, 'Tell me I'm a dumb bitch and you want to fuck some sense into my dirty, slutty cunt.'

Sorrowfully, he says, 'You're the most wonderful woman in the world and I want to make sweet, sweet love with you.'

Kissing him on the forehead while looking at me, she says, 'He's lovely, isn't he?' She takes a big gulp of wine. 'It's great when Andy makes love with me. It's the most amazing feeling of closeness to the person I love more than anything in this world. But ....'

'There are times when you want to try something a bit different.'

'Yes. And one of the things I like is being called names.'

I feel a wave of affection for her which is tied in with nostalgic thoughts. Fiona is the only other woman I've met who shares this fetish, but I try to make it sound like there's nothing unusual about it. 'I've known a number of women who like to be called "dirty whore" or "cheap slut," and I've met women who like to call the man "bastard" or "nasty fucker."'

'So, the tender act of love degenerates into two people screaming abuse at each other?' says Andy.

'Yes,' I say, 'and I have no issue with this. It doesn't change my opinion of the woman in any way. Once the excitement's over, we go back to speaking in civil terms. There's no malice behind the words, so I'm not bothered by them.'

Jenna nods in agreement, then says, 'It's not only that.' Despite her commitment to talking freely, she looks sheepish as she says, 'There are times when I ... want to hurt. I've occasionally persuaded Andy to spank me. He gives me a light pat on the butt and goes into a guilt trip like he's thrown me through a window.'

Andy sighs. 'I know they say you always hurt the one you love, but ....'

'But if she *wants* to be hurt ....' I leave this idea hanging and ask Jenna, 'What else do you like?'

She looks at Andy and they both smirk. 'What *doesn't* she like?' says Andy, shaking his head, in loving exasperation.

She keeps her eyes on me, looking to see how I react. 'He's right. I've never seen why people need to pigeonhole themselves as subs or doms, bondage freaks or water sports enthusiasts, when it's *all* such good fun!'

I look at Andy. 'But not so much fun for you.'

Shaking his head, he says, 'Oh, I'm sure it's fun. It's just I love Jenna so much ....'

I know what he means. I'm not always called in because the husband is lacking in bed or because the couple is turned on by the wife's infidelity. She could have a certain fantasy he can't bring himself to fulfil. I can see why. I've seen enough married couples over the years to know that the relationship between husband and wife is a complicated one. They support each other through the worst times. Each has seen the other cry. They're also business partners – joint managers of a home. If they have kids, he gives her the respect due to the mother of his children, while she admires him as a good father. With so many layers to the relationship, it's hard for one to see the other as a sexual being. Can you really ask your wife's advice on income protection insurance minutes after you've spanked her and called her a naughty girl?

Take one example. There was this couple, Thomas and Maria. I encountered them back in the day when I'd still meet people for the first time in their homes. They were two attractive, professional people in their late thirties, living in a house I could never afford. I arrived at the appointed time of six in the evening. Thomas answered the door and directed me to an armchair in their front room. He sat next to Maria on the couch. 'I wasn't sure you'd get here,' he said. 'The traffic's a nightmare.'

'Road works on the main street,' I said.

'Oh, you came that way? It's better to come by Milton Road. It can take ten minutes off your journey.'

'I'll remember that,' I said, trying not to smile.

Not many men feel comfortable saying, 'Hello, welcome, my wife's over here if you'd like to fuck her.' I always enjoy a cuckold's small talk while he tries to screw his courage to the sticking place. I glanced over at Maria, who also looked amused. I decided I'd get straighter talk out of her. 'What would you like to happen this evening?' I asked her.

'It's a little embarrassing,' she said, in a refined accent. A lot of money had been spent on sending her to a good school. I was intrigued to find out what dark secrets would be revealed in that cut glass voice of hers. 'I've always wanted a man to … pee on me.'

I nodded as if this was no big deal and turned to Thomas. 'It's something you do several times a day anyway, so why can't you do it for your wife?'

Shaking his head, he said, 'We've tried. Every time, I get a terrible case of shy bladder. Maria's lying in the bath, holding her boobs toward me, telling me how much it would turn her on. I'm pointing my prick at them, willing something to come out, and I can't squeeze out a drop.'

'Why do you think that is?'

He puffed out his cheeks. 'When I go out with her, she's always exquisitely dressed. She looks amazing, the very picture of an elegant woman. I can't reconcile that with someone who wants to be pissed on like she's a piece of trash.'

'We also tried it the other way round,' said Maria. 'It wasn't exactly what I wanted, but I figured it would be something. I found I had the same problem. Thomas is a respected doctor – a skin specialist. He's one of the few men I know who really helps people. It's hard to treat him as a toilet.'

'So … we were wondering if you could …' said Thomas.

I smiled at Maria. 'You want me to pee on you?'

Thomas coughed. 'If you could accommodate *both* of us, it would be much appreciated.'

This was a development I hadn't expected. 'You can do it, then walk away and forget about us,' said Maria.

I shrugged. 'I should tell you I haven't done this before, but I guess it'll be okay.'

As soon as she heard that, Maria nodded and went out of the room. She came back a moment later, carrying a tray. On it were a bottle of water, a pint of beer and a large mug of black coffee. 'These should help,' she said, putting the tray on the floor by my feet. Even in those days, I preferred not to drink on duty, but I figured one pint of beer wouldn't affect my judgement, so I downed it first. I drank the water more slowly and finished with the coffee. 'Are you ready?' she asked. I nodded. I wasn't desperate, but I figured I'd be able to go. There'd be a stage wait before we got started – time enough for my bladder to reach its full capacity.

We went upstairs and into their bathroom, where they took their clothes off. She was confident about her body, and I could see why. Despite having had a couple of kids, she had plump but firm breasts and a flat stomach. I didn't see her pussy as it was hidden behind a thick bush of brown hair. Her long legs elegantly stepped over the side of the bath. Kneeling down with her hands on her knees, she watched her husband take a lot longer over his undressing. I could understand why he was the self-conscious one. Men often feel uncomfortable getting naked in the locker room. It's even harder to take your clothes off in front of a man who's known to be highly-skilled in the sexual arena. In truth, Thomas didn't have much to worry about. He had a pretty good body, neither too fat nor too thin, a fine hairy chest and a good-sized cock. He wasn't fully erect. I guessed he was too anxious to give himself over fully to excitement. Even with a semi, he could show a good six inches – nothing to be ashamed of. Climbing into the bath, he knelt next to his wife. It was touching to see them link hands – mutually supportive at all times. Looking up at me, he asked, 'What do you want us to do?'

'This is a first for me too,' I reminded them.

'Why don't we tell you where we want it?' suggested Maria. She bit her lip as she had a naughty idea, 'Or we could tell you where to aim on each other.'

'As you wish,' I said, mildly.

'Show Thomas what you think of his penis,' she said.

Aiming my cock at his, I relaxed my muscles. Fortunately, my bladder was less susceptible to stage fright than Thomas's and I produced a strong, steady flow. Thomas pushed his crotch toward me, so I had more to aim at. I didn't want to use it all up on him, so I tensed my muscles and had a painful moment as I pointed my cock at Maria while looking at Thomas. 'Breasts,' was all he said.

I peed over Maria's tits, directing the stream to make sure all of them were covered. I paused again, still feeling like I had more in me. The beer and coffee were working their magic. 'Mouth,' said Maria.

I wanted to check Thomas was happy with this. As I turned back to him, I raised an enquiring eyebrow. He nodded and opened his mouth. I aimed for his tongue. He didn't close his mouth or make any attempt to swallow, preferring to let it run down his chin.

I reckoned I had enough in me for one more target, so I turned back to Maria. It was no surprise when Thomas said, 'The same.' She willingly opened her mouth. The pressure of my piss was dropping, so I had to step forward. She didn't stick out her tongue, so I had to aim deeper into her mouth. She swallowed as much as she could.

When my flow was down to a mere dribble, I tensed again and went over to their toilet to wipe myself. Looking back at Thomas and Maria, I saw them gazing at each other in surprise as if asking, *Did that really happen?* After a moment, they burst out laughing which is, I suppose, your only option when you've let a stranger pee on you. Thomas turned on the shower attachment and tenderly cleaned his wife. She took the attachment from him and washed his crotch, chin, and chest. Stepping out of the bath, they dried themselves off.

I hoped the foreplay was complete and that we'd move into the bedroom so I could fuck Maria. Or I was happy to do it right there on the bathroom floor. But Thomas stepped forward and shook my hand. 'I can't thank you enough. It's been a good experience for us.'

I realized that was a dismissal. Disappointed, I put my clothes on. Soon, I was back in my car, feeling antsy, like I had an unscratchable itch. Peeing over Maria had been a turn-on. It wasn't something I wanted to do every day, but it could certainly be thrown into the mix from time to time. Peeing on Thomas hadn't been as strange as I'd expected. After all, a key part of my role as bull, whether acknowledged or not, is the humiliation of the cuckold. Normally, this is done simply by showing my physical and sexual superiority. On this occasion, I had shown my dominance in a different way. I'd be happy to do it again if any man asks.

I wanted to cum. A true bull considers masturbation beneath his dignity, so I took out my phone. 'Hi, Paula, are you and Ray free tonight? Okay if I come over?'

'We're sitting down to dinner,' she said. 'If you're quick, you can join us.'

'On my way,' I said.

'Cards on the table time,' says Jenna. 'I like you. What do you think of me?'

'I think you're great,' I say, sincerely.

Jenna turns to Andy, who nods almost imperceptibly. It seems this is the signal Jenna needs. Turning back to me, she says, 'So, would you be horrified if we invited you back to our place?'

'If by "horrified," you mean "delighted," then yes, I would.'

Taking another gulp of wine, she looks at me with wicked eyes and asks, 'So, what do you want to do to me?'

It would sound wrong to say, 'I only want to give you pleasure.' Add the word "mistress" and I'd sound like a submissive. So, I dress it up by saying, 'I want to enjoy every part of your body. I want to take it slow and make you feel what you've never felt. I want you to know you've been fucked like never before.'

'Doesn't sound so bad,' she says, slowly. 'But … the first time, don't you want to bend me over a table and fuck me nasty until I can't walk straight?'

This isn't what I want to do, but I nod and say, 'That's also an option.'

'And … how do you see my role in this?' asks Andy.

It's a question I've heard before. It's fairly clear what the bull and the hot wife are going to do. The role of the cuckold isn't so well-defined. 'It's largely up to you. You can sit on the sidelines and watch if you want to. Or you can join in. Some women like the idea of being pleasured by two men.'

Jenna makes a noise in her throat indicating she *does* like this idea. Andy purses his lips, suspiciously, and asks, 'Join in how?'

It's time to acknowledge one of the biggest elephants in the room when talking about cuckoldry.

A guy will often fantasize about watching his wife or girlfriend with a woman. The porn industry perpetuates the myth that all women are bisexual and fool around with each other until a cock arrives. This is not the cuckold fantasy. A cuck wants to see his woman with another *man* and often goes into great detail about the qualities that man should have. 'I want to see you with a guy who's better-looking than me, and a whole lot stronger. He picks you up in his muscular arms and throws you down on the bed. When he gets his cock out, it's so beautiful you want to cry. It's twice as long as mine and so much thicker.'

The cuckold finds himself admiring this example of hyper-masculinity who's appeared in his bed. Ask any cuck to describe his wife's bull and he will be able to describe every detail of the stud's body, including his cock. Now, the cuckold might justify this to himself by saying it's just masochism. He wants to be humiliated by seeing his woman having better sex with another man than she's ever had with him.

But there *is* a sexual bond between the bull and the cuck, which can take many forms. Sometimes, there's a distance between the two men because they've all agreed the cuckold shouldn't be present while the woman is with her stud. This was my experience with Ava and Toby. I met them in a café beforehand and they were equally enthusiastic, but Toby didn't want to watch. She got into my car and I drove off as Toby waved us goodbye. Ava was nice-looking, with bright hazel eyes and a warm smile. I had no doubt we'd have a good time together, and we did. She was a bit hesitant when we arrived at my place. 'Is it okay if I … spend a bit of time … using my mouth?' she asked.

I was already semi-hard, so I unzipped my trousers and took out my cock. She gave a little gasp when she saw it – not an uncommon reaction – and got down on her knees. To be honest, her technique wasn't great. She'd made the mistake of thinking fellatio is like trying to suck an ice cube up a straw. Still, it's always nice to put your cock in a married woman's mouth, so I enjoyed it. I didn't let it go on too long, though, and soon had her naked on the bed. She had big, soft tits and thighs. She also had a shaven pussy, which I licked for a couple of minutes. We fitted together nicely, and I enjoyed fucking her. I had no difficulty bringing her to orgasm and I came over her belly. She put her clothes on and went home to Toby soon afterwards.

It was a good encounter – thoroughly enjoyable for both of us, but not exceptional. I wouldn't have been surprised if I'd never heard from her again, but I was pleased when she called me two days later and asked if she could come over. When she got to my place, the first question I asked her was, 'Did you tell Toby about last time?'

'Of course,' she replied, with a grin.

'How did he react?' You might think a bull would care about his own pleasure and – possibly – the woman's, without taking an interest in the cuckold. But I want all three interested parties to enjoy it.

Laughing, she said, 'He loved it. I edged him for hours.'

This was a new one on me. 'Edged?'

She raised her eyebrows. 'You've never been edged?' Looking at me, she said, 'No, probably not. When I got home, I showed him your cum on my tummy. He said, "I want to hear absolutely everything," so I took him to bed and we both got naked. He wanted to know what we talked about in the car, what your place was like, what happened in each room. I rubbed his dick all the time we were talking and it didn't take long to get him to the point where he was just about to cum.' Smiling proudly, she said, 'I kept him at that point for over an hour, as I told him every little detail of what you and I had been up to. After I finally let him cum, he said it was the most erotic experience of his life.'

'That's great,' I said. I meant it too. I was genuinely pleased my actions had given a man so much sexual pleasure. 'We'd better give him something else to get edged to.'

'I think we should,' she said, and headed to the bedroom.

The most common involvement of the cuckold is as spectator. I find it hard imagine what this is like. As far as I know, neither of my girlfriends cheated on me, so I've got no personal experience of a partner having sex with another man. It's the ultimate fantasy of so many guys. It took me a while to get used to having an audience. Sex is normally a private activity. Even if you're at an orgy or a party that's going well, the other people in the room are too busy having their own sex to look at you. Cuckoldry is different. The bull is under scrutiny all the time. Two people are expecting him to deliver a special experience and the pressure can be intense.

I sometimes feel as if I'm the object of the couple's personal show-and-tell, as the woman says, 'Look how big his cock is, darling,' and, 'Can you see how well he's fucking me?'

I quickly got used to the man's presence. The only time it bothers me now is when the man gets a sudden change of heart just as I'm penetrating his wife and tries to stop me. The woman's reaction when this happens varies. She might have to reassure him – probably for the hundredth time – 'Don't worry, my love, this isn't going to cause any problems between us. It'll just give us some hot stuff to talk about next time we're in bed.' But if she's so horny she doesn't care about anything except my cock, she might tell her beloved to sit down and shut up before looking into my eyes and saying, 'Forget about that loser and fuck me.' Now, you might think that's all I need. Technically, you're right: she's the only one who has to give consent. But I want everyone to be on board. including the man.

The bull is, almost by definition, dominant. I'm not sure the idea of a submissive bull is a contradiction in terms, exactly, but I've never heard of it. Part of this dominance is establishing himself as the alpha male over the cuckold. Cucks often fall naturally into a subordinate role, fetching drinks for his wife and her new beau. I've even known one who folded my clothes as I was fucking his wife.

Others need – or want – to be put in their place. This is often done verbally. 'Your wife needs me to fuck her, because you can't. Now watch and learn.' A visual aid can be used to emphasize this point. 'Look at my big cock. It's about to go deep inside your wife and you're going to watch it happen.'

Occasionally, a couple has a fantasy about the bull proving his *physical* dominance over the cuckold. I go along with this if it's important to them, but never enjoy it much. While I'm a big fan of sex, I don't care much for violence, and I don't know why they get lumped together. It's not too bad if the couple just wants a bit of wrestling. I'm stronger than most cucks and I've learned a few moves over the years. I usually grab his shoulders, sweep his legs from under him, and control his descent to the floor, where I easily pin him. It shows everyone who's boss, but no one gets hurt.

Then there was Tania and Stephen. They were into bruises. I don't know if that's a recognized thing or not. When they told me about it, I thought it was weird, and might have walked away if Tania hadn't been so attractive. She had ash blonde hair and piercing blue eyes. Her body was slim, but with nicely rounded breasts and butt. I wanted her as soon as I saw her, and wasn't going to let an unusual fetish spoil that. When we got to their place, Stephen wasted no time in taking all his clothes off. Waving his hand over his upper chest, he said, 'Plenty of nice bruises, but let's not crack any ribs, eh?' The problem was I had no idea how hard a punch was needed to do this. My first hits were mere taps. I increased the force until the first bruise appeared. I then moved along Stephen's chest, trying to repeat that force of punch. After a good deal of trial and error, he had the row of contusions that meant so much to them. I hoped, with that out of the way, we could get on with the important business of me fucking Tania. She was sitting on the couch, and had let out a low, ecstatic moan every time her husband was hit. He went over and showed her the bruises proudly, like they were medals for gallantry. Breathing heavily, she pressed her fingers into the sore parts. He winced every time, but they kissed passionately as she was doing it, and he had an impressive erection. It looked like my part in the proceedings was over and they were going to have sex. I think *he'd* have been quite happy with that, but she set him straight. 'I don't want to fuck the bruised man. I want to fuck the bruiser.' She walked over and kissed me. 'Thank you for hurting my husband,' she said.

'It was a pleasure,' I replied.

I said that only to be polite, but she misinterpreted it. 'Did you enjoy it as much as we did? Do you want to do it again?'

'I want to do you first,' I said, bending her over the couch and fucking her from behind. After we'd both cum, I made my excuses and left before they could suggest any further assaults on Stephen's person.

I also had the experience of a couple who wanted me to punish both of them. They lay on the bed together and I had two naked butts smiling up at me. They even had a cane they'd bought specially for the occasion. I laid into both of them, with the woman complaining if she thought I was being more gentle on her. After that, I didn't hold back and, by the time I'd finished, all four buttocks were a mess of red stripes, bruises, and a little blood. They both looked proud of themselves and they had the camaraderie of soldiers coming back from a mission. *It was tough, but we got through it together.*

Then there are the couples who dream of the bull establishing his sexual dominance by fucking both of them. I must admit I've never done this myself. I'm going on what I heard when chatting with a fellow bull.

I can't claim there's much community spirit between bulls. We don't get together every year for a Christmas party. I talked to Carl because he was relocating for work and had to leave his cuckold couple, Jane and Duncan, behind. They were looking for a replacement bull and he wondered if I'd be interested. He explained what happened when he visited them. As soon as he got through their front door, both of them fell to their knees in front of him and kissed his shoes. Duncan said, 'Thank you for wasting your time on us. We know we don't deserve it.' Carl didn't say anything, playing the part of the cold, silent fucker.

Jane stood up and showed Carl the sexy underwear she was wearing for him. 'If you're pleased by what you see, maybe you'd consider fucking me.'

They went upstairs. Carl told me that the actual sex was quite vanilla. They experimented with different positions, but Jane showed no interest in being dominated in bed, despite the deferential way she and her husband talked. Carl always wore a condom and came inside her. After that, Jane thanked him for fucking her and said she hoped she'd been satisfactory. Duncan also thanked him and brought him a glass of rum and Coke, Carl's favorite drink.

They left him alone for half an hour while he regathered his forces. There was a TV in their bedroom, so he channel-surfed while sipping his drink. Then the door opened and Jane came in, dragging Duncan behind her. Duncan was much bigger than Jane and could easily have resisted, but somehow, he didn't. 'I know I didn't please you,' said Jane. 'Maybe my husband can do better.'

Duncan lay down on his stomach and spread his buttocks to present Carl with a well-greased anus. Carl put on another condom and fucked Duncan. He said there were anatomical differences, but, essentially, it was the same process of having sex.

Carl told me that the *forced bi* fetish is growing in popularity and that, in reality, there's nothing forced about it. He'd discussed the situation extensively with Jane and Duncan before their first sexual encounter, when he was still allowed to speak. Their fantasy was of a man breaking into their married life and assuming total sexual control over both of them.

I decided not to become Jane and Duncan's new bull, as I sensed hints of sexism or homophobia in Carl's story. The message to Duncan seemed to be, *You think you're a red-blooded heterosexual male, but you're being forced to take on the role of a woman or a gay man.* I wasn't comfortable with that, so I walked away.

'I think the first time I'd rather just watch,' says Andy.

'Fine by me,' I say.

'Everything's fine by us, too,' says Jenna. 'So ... shall we go?'

We stand up and walk out of the bar. I go and sit in my car. A minute later, a blue Ford Focus drives by slowly and Jenna's hand appears through the passenger side window, beckoning me to follow. After a fifteen minute drive, they turn into an underground car park beneath a large apartment block. I follow them down and park in the space next to theirs. 'You'll be fine there,' says Andy, getting out of the car. 'Tim's away for the weekend.'

We take the elevator in silence. Jenna puts her hand in mine and gives it an excited squeeze. When we arrive at the top floor, Andy unlocks their front door. 'Welcome to our humble abode.'

There's nothing humble about this place. Looking out of the window, I see lights reflecting off the dark water of the Thames. An apartment like this with a view of the river does not come cheap. I didn't think to ask what they do, but they must have a bit of money behind them.

We're in a long, narrow room, warmly illuminated by flush lights on the walls. Opposite the front door is a small kitchen area. There's a dining table in front of the kitchen counter. The surfaces all look a bit too clean and new, like they don't get used much.

Putting his keys on the counter, Andy takes a bottle of wine out of the fridge and opens it. Cuckolds do this to preserve the illusion of entertaining a regular guest who's come round for a drink and a chat. I only take a polite sip. I'm already scoping out the lie of the land. We're in a living room dominated by a big, flat screen TV and a three-seater couch. This looks well-worn. I deduce that Jenna and Andy like to order in and eat in front of the TV. There's room for two to lie on the couch. Or I could bend Jenna over the pristine table and fuck her from behind, like she suggested. There's also an armchair, but I dismiss this. I could sit on it comfortably, but the arms would get in her way if she tried to ride my cock. The maroon carpet is soft and springy under my feet. It would be no hardship to screw her on the floor. However, I see a bedroom through one of the open doors leading off the main room. The double bed looks sturdy. That would be *my* ideal place. But a nice, soft bed might not fit in with her desire to be fucked nasty.

She puts down her glass and comes over to me. Draping her arms around my shoulders, she looks up at me. I naturally lower my face toward hers. Taking a step back, she says, 'We forgot to mention that. Do you mind if we don't kiss on the lips? That's for my boyfriend.'

I feel a stab of disappointment. She has a beautiful mouth and I've been looking forward to kissing it all evening. I tell myself it's her choice and we're still going to have a great time together. Putting my hand on her left breast, I caress it through her shirt. 'Please don't!' says Andy, in an urgent voice.

I wonder if this is another restriction they've agreed on and I look over at him. He's sitting on the couch, with eyes wide and mouth half-open. He hasn't got his cock out, but he's stroking a large bulge through his trousers.

'Touch my tits,' says Jenna, in a low voice. 'Don't worry about him.'

I deduce that I should follow all instructions from *her*, while ignoring what *he* says. I turn back to Jenna, who's unbuttoning her shirt. She gives me a look that's impish but not at all nervous. She knows what she's doing is naughty. She also knows I'm going to like what she's about to show me.

And I do. The skin on her shoulders is pale with a dusting of freckles. She's wearing a pink bra, which shows off four inches of cleavage but, otherwise, keeps its secrets well. However hard I look, I can't tell anything about the size or shape of her nipples. All I know is I'd like to bury my face between her tits during sex and fall asleep on them afterwards.

She pushes her breasts toward me. I cup my hands around them and squeeze gently. 'You're touching my tits,' she says. I already knew that, but I appreciate that, for her, saying it has an erotic charge equal to doing it. 'And me, a respectable engaged woman. I should not be doing this.' She gets over these qualms quickly and, putting her hands behind her back, undoes the fastening of her bra. She rounds her shoulders and the bra falls into her hands.

The first sight of her tits makes my mouth fall open. The dark line of her cleavage leads down to a triangle where her breasts separate. They have the heavy fullness of large boobs, but also the prominent red nipples and dark areolae normally associated with small tits. I know she wants me to say mean things about her, so I look at them with the most critical eye I can manage. I cannot see a single fault with them. 'Beautiful, perfect,' I say – not exactly stinging insults.

'Andy likes them too,' she says, with a smile. 'He'll have to get used to sharing them.'

A low moan from Andy indicates that he's coping well so far.

She unbuttons her jeans. Smart enough to leave her panties on, she stands in front of me, still with the confident smile of a woman who knows she'll be appreciated. I notice a blue and white butterfly tattooed over an appendectomy scar.

I've nothing against women with tattoos. I have huge admiration for the artists who can do such intricate work on a flinching canvas. I even like the crudely-drawn amateur tattoos, but for a different reason. The ones done by a drunk ex-boyfriend are cheap and ugly, making the woman look dirty and slutty. There are times when I appreciate a classy lady. Other times, I want to be with a skanky ho. There was only one tattoo on a girl that I didn't like. She had a realistic spider on her left forearm. I'm not the world's biggest fan of spiders. If it had been a big, hairy tarantula, I wouldn't have reacted the same way. My brain would have told me there aren't many tarantulas running loose in Britain, so it couldn't be real. But her tattoo was a faithful representation of critters I'd seen in my bath, and I jumped every time she took her clothes off.

I kneel in front of Jenna. (Yes, I do remember what I said earlier, but … shut up.) I'm nervous as I move my head toward her. What am I scared of? Am I going to be like a virgin and shoot my load on first contact with a pussy? I tell myself not to be stupid: I didn't do that even when I *was* a virgin. I kiss her cunt through her panties and inhale deeply. The scent of her pussy is intoxicating. The clean cotton freshness of her panties is like a drop of water in a fine whiskey. It only enhances the complex aroma.

I don't cum immediately, but there's a danger I will soon if I keep kissing her pussy, so I stand up. Jenna looks me in the eye and says, 'Daniel, you and I are going into the bedroom. Andy can join us or not. Right now, I don't care. I'm going to get on all fours on the bed and you are going to screw me from behind. It'll be hard and rough. You're going to treat me like the whore I am. You will fuck your little slut.'

I don't know if this talk is meant primarily to turn on me or Andy. He's groaning loudly and stroking his crotch so hard, there's a danger he'll rub a hole in his trousers. I *should* love what she's saying. Ever since I split from Fiona, I've been looking for a woman who loves name-calling. Now I've met one, I don't want to say mean things to her. I don't want to call her a whore. I want to tell her she's beautiful and sexy.

I'm not even sure I want to fuck her. I think I might want to – don't say it, Daniel! – *make love* to her.

The thoughts roiling through my head are making me seasick. I must focus. A woman I find supremely attractive is laying out her plans for me to have hot sex with her. This is not an opportunity I want to miss.

It looks like I *will* miss it. My erection should be like a drill bit, ready to explore her. But it's not. I can feel it's small and wrinkled like … well, like a cuckold's dick. Andy's frowning. He senses there's a problem. So, does she. 'Is everything okay, Daniel?' she asks.

I can't believe I'm delivering the cuckold's excuse. 'I don't know what's wrong. This has never happened before.'

She smiles. 'Don't worry, baby.' She pauses before asking, 'Did I do anything you didn't like?'

'No, you're great. You've no idea how much I want to do this, but ….'

'If it doesn't happen, it doesn't happen,' she says, soothingly. 'Either way, we're both glad we met you.'

Don't be nice, Jenna! Act like a bitch! If I didn't like you so much, I might be able to fuck you.

Andy doesn't help by saying, 'Maybe we should have a drink and try again later.' It would also help if I could hate him. I'd feel as if I was teaching a cuckold a lesson. But I like him too. I don't want to hurt him. I want …. Oh, fuck! I want to *be* him.

I have to get out of here. I still have all my clothes on, so this is easy enough – logistically, if not emotionally. Mumbling my apologies, I head for the door. They both look worried, like I'm a friend who's acting strangely and they're not sure why. Jenna's still standing there in nothing but her panties. I know what will happen as soon as I've left. Despite their obvious concern for me, enough has happened this evening to leave them in an advanced state of arousal. They'll make love while talking about what Jenna had been only too keen to do, even if it hadn't worked out.

I leave without another word. I start down the stairs but don't make it to the first landing. I sit down heavily and stare at the wall.

It's a nondescript brown wall, which doesn't warrant more than a second's glance. I look at it for a full five minutes, finding it hard to form a coherent thought. After a couple of minutes, I heave myself up and go downstairs. Once in my car, I breathe heavily. I need someone to talk to and take out my phone. 'Hi, Paula, it's Daniel. Could I come over and *not* have sex with you?'

She laughs. 'Sure, if you want. I won't force myself on you.'

When I arrive at their house, Paula and Ray have the same worried frowns I saw on the faces of Jenna and Andy. As I sit down, Ray puts a hand on my shoulder and says, 'How can we help?' I'm reminded again of how much I like this guy. There aren't many husbands who would behave like this to the man who's fucked his wife hundreds of times.

Paula makes tea, and we sit in their front room. I'm not sure how to begin. 'Do you watch boxing?' I ask them, at last.

Ray looks confused. He wasn't expecting a manly talk about sports. 'I'm not a big fan, but I have done.'

'Have you ever seen someone who used to be a great fighter but now isn't the man he was? It's time for him to retire so we can remember him at his best. Well, I'm no boxer, but I do have a talent.'

Paula grins. 'You don't have to tell me. If you're talking about what I think you're—'

'I am,' I tell her, firmly. 'I was with a couple tonight.' I'm not sure if I should tell them I was with their friends. I don't want Paula to feel like I'm blaming her for setting me up with them. 'They're both nice. I wanted her in the worst way but ....'

'The little soldier didn't report for duty,' says Ray. I hate the sympathy in his eyes. No cuckold should ever feel sorry for a bull. Worse than that, though, is the look of fellow feeling, as he says, 'It happens to all of us.'

Not to me, it doesn't, I think, but don't say. *That's why I'm a bull.*

'I'm sure a boxer wouldn't hang up his gloves after losing one fight,' says Paula.

'It's not just that,' I say. I stop and stare at the carpet for a moment. What I'm about to reveal is more of an embarrassment than my failure to have sex. 'This woman's different. I think I might be ….' I trail off, realizing it could be insensitive to talk like this in front of Paula.

Fortunately, she realizes what I'm saying. 'It's okay, Daniel. I'm fond of you and I enjoy our times together, but I love Ray. All three of us know that's not going to change. I won't get jealous if you fall for someone else.'

Ray leans forward and gives me a *Let's talk man-to-man* look. 'Daniel, if you have feelings for this woman, maybe you should tell her. Who knows, she might feel the same way about you?'

'How can she? We only met this evening.'

'It was enough for you,' Paula points out.

I shake my head. 'One of the great freak occurrences of our time. It couldn't happen twice.'

'You think you're the only person in history to fall in love at first sight?' asks Ray, gently teasing.

'Anyway, I can't talk to her about it.'

'Why not?'

I pause. It feels like breaking the seal of the confessional. 'Because it's Jenna. As in Jenna and Andy.'

Ray understands immediately. 'I see what you mean. There's not much point in telling her.'

Paula nods in agreement. 'I was going to ask how that went. But Ray's right, you'll never get between those two.'

'I wouldn't want to. They're great together.' I sigh. 'It goes against everything a bull's supposed to do. A couple should be able to bring a stud into their life, safe in the knowledge he won't mess things up. The job of the bull is to come in, fuck the woman, and leave without emotions getting in the way.'

Paula leans back and looks up at the ceiling. 'Are you sure it's Jenna herself?' she asks.

'What do you mean?' I ask, frowning.

'You see how much Jenna and Andy care for each other. Maybe you want to be that close to someone.'

'That's like telling a committed vegetarian he might fancy a nice steak,' I reply.

She nods. 'You've always said you could never go back to a normal relationship, but maybe—'

I interrupt her. 'Saturday afternoons spent holding bags while my girlfriend tries on clothes? Dinner parties with David and Amanda?'

'Who are they?' asks Ray.

'I don't know, but when you're part of a couple, you inevitably hang out with people who have names like David and Amanda.'

'I don't think it's compulsory,' says Paula. Putting her hands behind her head, she looks deep in thought. 'Ray,' she says, at last, 'what about Christa?'

He nods. 'That's what I was thinking.'

'Who's Christa?' I ask.

At four o'clock the next afternoon, I take the Underground to Tottenham Hale and make my way to a large redbrick townhouse. I don't have any qualms about going to Christa's home for our first meeting. I'm simply here to have a chat with one of Paula and Ray's friends, so the normal rules don't apply. I ring the bell and, as I wait for a reply, step back and look up at the house. I guess it has at least five bedrooms. This isn't a fashionable area of London but, even so, you wouldn't get much change from half a million at today's prices.

A voice says, 'Jamie's grandfather bought this house a hundred years ago. It's been in the family ever since. Not a bad place to be.' A woman in her late twenties is standing in the doorway. Her brown hair is short, in a style perilously close to being a pixie cut. She has deep brown eyes, a straight nose, and a thin but amiable smile. I have the curious feeling all she'd have to do is change her haircut and she'd be a good-looking man. She's also wearing a masculine-looking combination of stonewashed jeans and a white t-shirt. She holds out her hand. 'You must be Daniel.'

I follow her as she goes back into the house. She leads me along the hallway and into the kitchen, which is cheerfully lit by the sun coming through the French windows. In the center of the room, there's a huge oval table in black stained oak. She points at one of the chairs and I sit down, while she puts the kettle on. When we've each got a steaming mug of tea in front of us, she asks, 'What did Paula say about me?'

'Not much,' I admit. 'Just that it would be worth talking to you.'

Christa nods. 'She told me a little about you. I hear you're quite the ladies' man.'

'That's one way of putting it.'

'You have no-strings-attached sex with married women. A lot of people would say you're living the dream.'

'So, would I, most of the time. But ... it's a young man's game.'

Looking me at me appreciatively, she says, 'And you with your pacemaker and Zimmer frame.'

'Give me a couple of years.'

'So, do what everyone else does. Get married, have two kids, spend Sunday morning washing your car.' She smirks. 'Go out to dinner with David and Amanda.'

'She told you that, did she? Did she also say I'd sooner die?'

'Pretty much. She reckons the set-up we have here might suit you better.'

'She didn't give any details.'

She takes a sip of her tea and backtracks. 'When I was eighteen, newly arrived at college, I fell heavily for this guy called Mike. He was the same way about me. We were everything to one another. It felt like a betrayal if we did anything with anyone else. He loved football, and I went to matches with him. A lot of Saturday afternoons were lost, watching guys running around a field. I did it to be with Mike. In fairness, he did things he didn't want to do, as well. I like karaoke, and he came along to a lot of nights and sat there, trying not to cringe. He even had a go a couple of times, picking a song like "I'm Too Sexy" that doesn't need a huge vocal range. Now, you might say those are the compromises you have to make in relationships.'

'No, I wouldn't. I'd say it's one of the main reasons I walked away from relationships.'

'Maybe a bit rash,' she says, gently. 'Three years ago, I met Jamie. He told me he likes to play video games on Tuesday nights.

I had a go at Pacman twenty years ago, and that was enough for me. But I resigned myself to spending every Tuesday evening doing something I don't like. Because it's what people do, right? But he told me he plays with his friends, Simon, Gary, and Bella. The games often go on into the night so I shouldn't wait up. At first, I was pissed off. *How dare he want to do anything without me?* But I realized I could spend Tuesdays doing whatever I wanted. It was a liberating moment when I said, "Go and have fun with your friends. I'll see you tomorrow."'

'So, you're in a relationship, but you also have friends,' I say. 'It's ground-breaking.' I don't want to offend her, so I make sure I smile broadly.

Fortunately, she smiles back. 'Every journey to an exotic place starts with a boring bus ride to the station. This was our first step in understanding that no one person can give you everything. The next was realizing that applies even in the bedroom. It's a huge mistake to expect one person to fulfil all your sexual needs. You'll never find anyone who shares every one of your kinks and predilections. For example, Jamie's into dressing up and role-play. He likes a woman to wear a nurse's uniform and perform intrusive procedures on him. I tried it, but couldn't keep a straight face. To me, there's something inherently funny about telling a guy I'm worried about his testicles and I need to give them a thorough examination. But Bella likes it as much as he does. She throws herself into the role with real commitment. She even read *An Introduction to Nursing* so she could use the right terminology. It's simply better if Jamie acts out that particular fantasy with her instead of me. And … speaking for myself … I'm into anal. I love the feel of a big, hard cock plugging up my tight, little asshole. Even more than the physical sensations, I enjoy the naughtiness of letting a man put his cock where it's not meant to be. Jamie doesn't like it. He says it's like crawling in through the cat flap rather than using the front door.'

'I guess you've found someone who ain't too proud to use the cat flap,' I say.

'Damian loves the cat flap.' Christa pauses and looks me in the eye. 'He also loves *me*. And I love him.'

'It's not all about sex, then.'

'What we're into is polyamory. Do you know what that is?'

'When you're in love with your parrot?' I suggest.

Rolling her eyes, she says sarcastically, 'I've never heard that one before. It means loving multiple people. This house is too big for Jamie and me, so others come and go. Damian stays over a few times a week. Sometimes he sleeps with me. Or he might bed down in the spare room. He and Jamie have become good friends. Bella's been living here for the last two months. Officially, she's looking for her own place, but she seems pretty comfortable where she is. And, that's fine. It's up to Jamie if he wants to be with her or me tonight. Or she and I might curl up together. We love each other too. We don't always fool around, but I'm happy to keep her warm at night. Other friends stay over from time to time. We couple up – or triple up – in whatever way feels most natural on the night. We have a jar in the kitchen. Everyone who stays over throws in a few pounds to help with the bills.'

A key turns in the lock and the front door opens.

'We're in the kitchen, babe,' calls Christa.

A guy in his early thirties comes in. He has reddy-brown hair and glasses that look specially made to match his hair color. He kisses Christa on the lips. Putting her arms around his neck, she kisses him back. 'Jamie, this is Daniel. He's a friend of Ray and Paula's.' He shakes my hand. 'Daniel's interested in our lifestyle.'

'It works for us,' he says, with a smile.

'Doesn't it just,' she agrees. 'Is Bella in for dinner?'

'As far as I know.' He takes a sip from Christa's teacup and heads for the door. 'I've got stuff to do. I'll leave you guys to it.'

After he's gone, I ask, 'Don't you ever get jealous, knowing your boyfriend's with another woman?'

'I don't call Jamie my boyfriend. I prefer to say he's my best friend. I did feel bad at first. I wondered what I was lacking. Wasn't I enough to satisfy a man by myself? Those feelings soon died. We *all* love each other. I would do anything for Jamie, or Damian, or Bella, and they'd do the same for me. That's not affected by who's in my bed at the time. We don't have any bullshit about *You're mine, so I control you.* They can do whatever they want. It won't change the way I feel about them.'

'So, if … one wanted to join your ….' I'm not sure what the right word is. '… collective?' I hazard.

'Group of friends.'

'How would one go about it?'

'Well, *one* would spend time with the group. Maybe *one* would stay to dinner tonight. We'd see how the rest of the guys took to *one*.' Biting her lip, she adds, 'It would help if you were sexually attracted to one or more of us.'

'I've only met you and Jamie so far.'

'Do you want to fuck Jamie?'

'Not so much.'

'It had better be me, then.'

I wasn't expecting this. I haven't felt the vibes, but I'm happy about this development. I've liked Christa more and more as we've been talking. This makes up for any lack of initial attraction.

She takes me upstairs and shows me into a room with two large single beds on opposite sides. The wallpaper looks like a relic from the 1970s – different shades of red and grey in a swirling pattern. Fortunately, most of it's hidden behind bookshelves and an eclectic collection of pictures – Japanese prints, a handsome portrait of a horse, comic book art. Jamie's lying on one of the beds, tapping at his phone. He looks up as we come in.

'I'm going to spend a bit of time with Daniel,' says Christa.

'Have fun,' says Jamie, and turns back to his phone. He couldn't be less interested if she said we were going to do our taxes.

She leads me to the bed that's against the opposite wall. We sit on the bed and she kisses me. My right hand moves up her side to her left breast. It's tiny, but something tells me she has a nipple worth nibbling. Her arms are around me. Making appreciative noises, she runs her fingers down my lats. She's getting into it, but

I'm struggling. Jamie's presence is putting me off. It's not that he's watching us. I'm used to that. It's that he's *not* watching. I glance over and see him chuckling at something on his screen. He might not call Christa his girlfriend, but she is his regular sexual partner. You'd think he'd be at least curious about what's happening on the other side of the room.

I tell myself to focus on the woman beside me. Maybe I need to see some skin. She raises her arms above her head and I pull her t-shirt off. She's wearing a white bra, which is unnecessary but cute. Slim but not toned, she clearly doesn't spend a lot of time in the gym, but isn't much interested in food. I like her body, but I can't feel any stirring in my trousers. Kissing her shoulder, I inhale deeply, hoping her feminine scent will flip a primitive arousal switch inside me. Still nothing. I stroke and squeeze her breasts, putting a finger under her bra so I can feel her nipple. As I thought, it's large and hard. I should be teasing it with my teeth right now.

At this rate, I'll have to ask her to touch my cock and try to massage life into it. No bull should ever need that. While these thoughts are sending me deeper into panic, she stands up, undoes her belt and steps out of her jeans. Her panties are in the same white material. She lies back on the bed. I kiss her thighs, enjoying their smooth softness. I can smell her cunt, and it's good. I'm painfully aware it *should* be turning me on.

What is wrong with me? I can't believe it's the hint of androgyny that's putting me off. In the past, I've fucked women who were a lot more mannish than Christa. I have to admit it's not that at all. I need to hear Jamie's heavy breathing as I show his woman what she's been missing out on. I want him to moan as he sees how much bigger and stronger than him I am. I'd give Christa a hundred pounds if she'd only shout, 'He's so much better than you, babe!'

I respect what these guys are doing. I like the idea of having total freedom within a framework of love and support. But it's not something I can do. Part of me wants to finish what I'm doing with Christa, so I don't feel I'm on a losing streak. But I can't. She's having sex with me on the understanding that I'm interested in being part of her group. If I've changed my mind, I'd be fucking her under false pretenses, and that wouldn't be right.

She realizes there's a problem. Raising her head, she asks, 'Are you okay, Daniel?'

'I'm fine,' I say, unconvincingly.

'Did I do anything you didn't like?'

I went twenty years without hearing that question. Now I've heard it twice in two days. 'No, Christa, you're great. I don't know what it is.'

Jamie has to choose this moment to take an interest. 'There are times when it just doesn't work,' he says, sympathetically.

Have I really got to the stage where men pity instead of envy me?

'I'm not sure this is for me,' I mumble.

'It's not for everyone,' says Christa, looking understanding rather than hurt or embarrassed.

Again, none of *my* clothes have come off, so I'm able to get out of the place quickly. I walk away from the house, feeling confused. Without my car, there's nothing to stop me having a beer in the pub at the end of the road. I find a quiet table and sit there, nursing my pint. I'm aware of girls checking me out, but I don't respond. Until I work out what I want, it's best I keep to myself.

To give me something to look at besides the table top, I pull out my phone and see if there are any messages. There's one from a number I don't recognize. This usually means a request for either personal training or sex. But this one says, *Hope you're OK. We both enjoyed meeting you and would love to see you again – even if it's just as friends. Love, Jenna.*

I look at this for a while before I text back, *Are you guys free now?* and send her my current location.

I spend half an hour deleting old messages. The door of the pub swings open and Jenna comes in, followed by Andy. She's wearing a simple white shirt with black trousers. She still knows she doesn't have to dress up in order to be wildly attractive. They both look worried. Sitting next to me, Jenna puts her arm around my shoulder and kisses my cheek. 'How are you, Daniel?' she asks.

Her touching me like a friend makes my stomach churn in a way that's both exciting and nauseating. Taking a moment to look at her, I ask myself again what it is about this woman that has got me questioning everything about myself. Is she the most beautiful woman I've ever seen? No. Is she the nicest person I've ever met? She's up there, but it's harder to compile a definitive ranking of niceness. By any objective standard, Christa's equally attractive and nice. So why didn't she have this effect on me? Maybe we never know why a particular person attracts us so much. If you'd asked Romeo what made Juliet different from all the other girls in Verona, he'd have shrugged and said, 'I don't know. Just something about her, I guess.'

Andy decides I need another drink and goes to the bar. He comes back with a beer for me and a white wine for Jenna. He doesn't have anything for himself, so I guess he's driving.

'I don't think I can just come round to your place and fuck you, Jenna,' I say.

It seems she didn't hear the word "just," because her face falls. 'You don't like me?'

I smile sorrowfully. 'The trouble is I like you too much.' I turn to Andy. 'The real bitch is I like you, as well.'

'Thanks,' he says, uncertainly. 'I like you. Not sure why it's a bitch.'

'If you were an asshole who didn't deserve her, I'd have no hesitation in stealing her away from you.' I realize this sounds presumptuous, so I turn to Jenna and add, 'Assuming you wanted to be stolen, of course. But you two are a great couple. I'd never do anything to spoil that.'

'So what ...?' he asks.

'I learned a word recently. *Polyamory*. Ever heard of it?'

Jenna nods. 'Loving multiple people.'

I look at Andy seriously. 'You have this fantasy where you watch another man fucking Jenna.' At the mere mention of this, his pupils dilate. 'What you adore so much is the idea of someone else being intimate with your fiancée.' He nods. I lean toward him and look him straight in the eye. 'But ask yourself this, Andy, how intimate is sex, when you get right down to it? Go to any town center on a Friday night, and you'll see people who have just met fucking against dumpsters. They have no feelings whatsoever for each other and do it out of simple convenience. Jenna could go out tonight and have sex with anyone she wanted.' She blushes at the compliment. 'If she did, sure, you'd have the thrill of knowing another guy had touched her in a way that should be reserved for you. How much more of a thrill would it be if you saw her being *emotionally* intimate with someone? You like the idea of her being unfaithful. What if she's being unfaithful with her heart as well as her body? Imagine you wake up in the morning and find Jenna sitting up in bed looking at her phone. She turns to you and says, "Morning, sweetie, just texting my boyfriend." You go into the cinema and Jenna's sitting on the back row with another guy. They're not touching, but they're sharing a tub of popcorn. He's making her laugh by whispering comments on the film into her ear. They're such a sweet couple, but one of them's Jenna and the other one isn't you. Wouldn't it drive you crazy? Now imagine she kisses another man, looks deep into his eyes and says, "I love you so much." Doesn't that make you feel like a *real* cuckold?'

He's breathing heavily and sweating a little. He likes the idea.

We're talking about Jenna like she's not here, and she is, after all, the most important person in this scenario. I ask her, 'How would you like to have a nice boyfriend and … a nasty boyfriend.'

'Obviously every girl dreams of having a nasty boyfriend,' she says, 'but … you're nice too.'

'Well … thank you,' I say, 'but maybe I'm nice in a different way. Andy looks at you and wants to protect you. You're like a lovely flower and he doesn't want to damage a single petal. I look at you and see – no offense – a kinky bitch.'

She giggles and takes a gulp of her wine. 'None taken.'

'I like you, which is why I want to make all your worst fantasies come true. I want to throw you down and fuck you senseless while calling you a dirty whore. I want to take you to your limits and spend time walking the tightrope between *It's all too much* and *It's never enough.'*

She takes my hand and places it against her chest. But, this isn't about touching her tits. She wants me to feel the thumping of her heart. 'The idea is not unappealing,' she says. 'But let's try to think straight for a moment. Andy and I are getting married soon.'

'It'll be a wonderful day. Everyone will be so happy for you. But imagine coming down the aisle with your new husband on your arm. You go into a little room to compose yourself and your boyfriend's waiting for you. How many women still have a boyfriend after they get married? I kiss you, tell you how proud I am of you, and how much I love you. Then, still in your wedding dress, you kneel down, and shatter your vows by taking my cock in your mouth.'

They both moan at this idea. Jenna's still trying to be rational. 'How's this … going to work? I mean, am I with you Mondays, Wednesdays and Fridays, then—'

I interrupt her. 'It'll work itself out. At times, you'll be with me. Other times, you'll be with Andy. There'll also be times when it's all three of us. We'll fall into patterns naturally. Remember, none of us is signing a lifelong contract here. If it doesn't work out, we can go our separate ways and no hard feelings.' Their eyes meet. This can't be agreed with one of their little nods. Standing up, I say, 'Could you guys excuse me a moment? I need the toilet.' They know as well as I do this is a pretext for leaving them alone. Nonetheless, I do go to the gents' and manage to squeeze out a few drops.

The door to the beer garden is next to the toilet so I step outside and get a bit of air while I wonder what the outcome will be. I don't think Jenna and Andy will take the opportunity to make a run for it. They're too polite. I do think it's possible Jenna will say, 'Sorry, Daniel, sex is one thing, but there's only one boyfriend for me.'

After five minutes, I take a deep breath and go back in. Sitting back down at the table, I raise an inquiring eyebrow. Jenna says, 'We've talked about it, and we honestly don't know if it'll work.

Relationships are complicated enough when there's just two of you.' She pauses and looks to Andy, who nods reassuringly. 'But we would like to give it a go.'

'Great,' I say, grinning broadly.

For a moment, I'm not sure what to do next. Fortunately, Jenna takes the lead. 'If you're my boyfriend, now, I suppose we'd better go home and do what boyfriends and girlfriends do.'

She stands up and holds out both her hands. Andy takes the right. I take the left. We walk out to their car together.

As soon as Andy closes their front door, the three of us go into the bedroom. Jenna lifts her face toward mine. We all know the kissing embargo has been lifted. My lips touch hers and a jolt of electricity goes through me. I must have kissed over two hundred women. It shouldn't be any more exciting than doing the laundry by now. But Jenna's lips feel so good. The ideal shape. The right degree of softness. There's wine on her breath but a sweet tanginess underneath which is all her. I *have* to explore her mouth with my tongue. We spend five minutes kissing passionately. My cock is pushing uncomfortably against the front of my trousers. I silently tell him that he'll need to give the performance of his life today. He tells me not to worry: he's going to be with me every step of the way. Holding Jenna's arms above the elbows, I move my lips down to kiss her neck. Her perfume is light and floral. There's also a natural scent, which suggests this girl would smell like new-mown hay if she never used another drop of perfume in her life. She tilts her head away from me as I land fleeting kisses over her throat. Unbuttoning her shirt, I expose her breasts. She's wearing a black bra, opaque, but with wispy lace trim. She takes a step back and looks at me with the same mischievous pride I saw before as she pushes the straps away from her shoulders. 'Do you like your girlfriend's tits?' she asks.

I thought the mere mention of the G word in this environment might cause my cock to shrivel, but I feel him still there. I tell him to be patient. I'm not going to rush this. By way of an answer to her question, I lift her tits up to feel their sensual heaviness. Taking her left nipple into my mouth, I suck it gratefully.

I lead her to the bed and gently lay her down. Still fully-clothed, I lie on top of her and kiss her again. 'What would turn you on most right now?' she asks. Her look is one of total confidence in herself as a sexual being. After things went wrong last time, you might expect her to be unsure of herself. But there's no doubt in her eyes. She knows it's going to work out fine this time.

Looking down at her, I say, 'You. Just you. You don't have to do anything. Let me get to know my girlfriend's body.'

Jenna lifts her head to kiss me on the cheek. 'It's all for you, babe.'

These words invoke one of Andy's low moans. He's leaning against the wall by the side of the bed. His cock's out and he's massaging it gingerly – *edging*.

I slide myself eight inches down the bed so my face is level with her breasts. Putting my lips around each nipple in turn, I suck gently. I lift up her left breast and lick its warm underside. There's a hint of sweet perspiration, which excites me. I kiss my way down her round, sensuous belly, until I arrive at the button of her trousers.

There is nothing sexier in the world than a woman lifting her butt off the bed to allow a man to remove her trousers. Jenna adds to it by saying, 'I want you to undress me. I want to be naked for you.'

I'm careful to leave her panties in place as I pull the trousers down her soft, smooth thighs. I want to tease myself. Her panties are powder blue. I love pale panties because they show the woman's arousal so clearly. Jenna has a large wet patch, which I have to kiss, inhaling deeply at the same time. Jenna's most intimate scent makes me as dizzy as it did the first time. It's the perfect combination of sweet, sour, and salty notes.

Putting two fingertips under the band of her panties, I lower them, one millimeter at a time. Below her panty line, she has a freckle, which I kiss tenderly. Pulling her panties down a few more millimeters reveals the first wisps of coppery hair. Slowly I reveal her neatly-trimmed bush. She reprises her butt lift move so I can finally remove her panties. As I pull them past her ankles, I notice how pretty her feet are. I'm no foot fetishist, but I can appreciate any well-turned part of a woman's body. I take each of her toes into my mouth in turn. This makes her smile instead of moan, so I deduce having her toes sucked is sensual rather than sexual for her.

For me, though, sucking her toes is self-teasing. I want her cunt so badly that I make myself wait, letting the desperation build. When I can't bear it anymore, I lie down between her legs, and use my thumbs to part her outer lips. I wonder if this is the moment I'll finally find something wrong. Will her inner lips be lopsided or too prominent? Will her prepuce bulge out or be squashed to one side?

I needn't have worried. Her pussy lips form two concentric coral ovals around the shiny white pearl of her clit and her burgundy vagina. I put my mouth on her clit and flicker the tip of my tongue over it. She tastes so good I have to lick her, lapping at her pussy like it's my favorite ice cream. 'Oh, yeah! Lick that cunt!' she says. I'm in danger of breaking my rule about using my tongue to excite a woman too much. Fortunately, she interrupts me by saying, 'Daniel, tell me what I am.'

Despite the way I feel about her, I'm sure of my role as nasty boyfriend now, so I look at her, and tell her with conviction, 'You're a dirty whore, Jenna. You're a cheap little tart for my big, black cock.'

She growls with dark pleasure and looks up at Andy. 'What do *you* say I am?'

'You're the most beautiful, wonderful woman in the world. I love you like I've never loved anyone before.'

She looks from him to me with a grin that says, *I've got it all.* Focusing on me again, she says, 'It's time to get to know my new boyfriend a bit better. Strip for me, Daniel. Slowly.'

I like that she shares my love of the gradual reveal. It's unfortunate that male stripping is often associated more with comedy than eroticism. I make sure there's nothing comical about the way I undo my buttons and take off my shirt, tensing my abs so they look at their best. I lay my shirt over the back of the chair by the bed and unbuckle my belt. I ease my trousers slowly down over my well-toned thighs. I expertly take off my shoes and socks as I remove my trousers. No man looks sexy with shoes and socks at the end of bare legs. She looks at me with raw lust in her eyes. I walk over to her. She stands up and meets me at the end of the bed. Working her way slowly down my body, she kisses my lips, my neck, and my pecs. Her tongue flicks my left nipple, making my shiver. Tracing her fingers over my abs, she moans softly as she feels how hard and defined they are. She takes a moment to bury her nose in my pubes and inhale my scent, before she has to change position. Kneeling down, she lifts my cock out of the way. My whole body tingles as I feel the touch of her lips on my balls. She kisses each one in turn and then starts licking. At first, she uses only short, fleeting strokes of her tongue. But soon, she's licking my whole sack, from the base of my scrotum to the root of my cock. Tenderly putting her lips around the head of my cock, she licks it with small, slow circles of her tongue. Her tongue is warm and moist. I remind myself not to get too excited. I'm sure she wouldn't mind if I came in her mouth, but that's not how I want this to end. I gently push her head away from me.

I'm about to lift her up and lay her on the bed, when she surprises me by saying, 'Andy, why don't you show Daniel how much you appreciate him?'

Both of us know what this means. Andy takes a moment. He looks at Jenna and sees she's too drunk with lust to worry about the consequences.

I'm more turned-on than I've been in years, but I can still be rational. Thinking about what's going to happen, I realize I've got no problem with it.

'Go on,' says Jenna, teasingly. 'What are you afraid of? It tastes good. Trust me, I know.' She runs her tongue around her lips.

Andy groans with desire at this taunt, but still hesitates.

'Remember,' she says, 'you're only doing it to turn *me* on. What's wrong with a man exciting his girlfriend?'

It seems this is what he needs to put the act into a context his brain can accept. He doesn't build up to it slowly the way she did. He has no urge to kiss my balls. He moves forward purposefully. He grabs my cock and stuffs it into his mouth – quickly, so he doesn't have time to think too much about it. I look down and it *is* odd to see a man's head clamped to my groin. I focus on Jenna. Her delight at what she's seeing confirms that we're doing this largely for her benefit. I'm not sure why this makes me feel better – and I'm not proud of this – but it does. In terms of physical sensation, it's not much different. Andy's clean-shaven, so it's not like there's a beard scratching against my thighs. I discover the inside of a man's mouth feels pretty much the same as a woman's.

I know this isn't about giving me pleasure. It's to establish my dominance over him. I tap him on the head as soon as I reckon the point's been made. It would be made more forcefully if I came in his mouth and made him swallow it. That's also not how I want this to end.

He pulls his head away and stands up. He doesn't look ashamed or embarrassed – just a little surprised. I've a good idea what he's going to do next, though. He kisses his girlfriend assertively, grabbing her breast at the same time. He's giving both of us the message, *I may just have sucked a man's cock, but I'm still straight.*

I must admit there's also part of me wants to reassert my heterosexuality. Lying on top of Jenna, I kiss her. I love that she kisses me with the same warmth and passion she has for Andy. I touch and kiss her breasts again – not for any particular reason, but because I find them irresistible. My cock is standing straight and hard. I'm proud of the way he's rallied after his recent run of bad form. A lesser cock would have been tentative and nervous.

Andy's standing by the bed. He hands me a condom – a simple act, but one which makes his subservience to me at this moment almost complete. Almost. I look up at him. 'Say it.'

He gulps before saying hoarsely, 'I love Jenna so much. Please don't fuck her.'

She gazes at him with real love in her eyes as she says, 'Shut up, Andy. He's going to fuck me better than you ever could.'

I take the condom from him and I'm on the point of tearing the packet when Jenna puts her hand on my arm. 'Have you always been safe?' she asks.

'Believe it or not, I have – more or less.' I reply.

'So have I,' she says. 'I'm on the pill, so don't worry – no little Daniels. I want to feel you cum inside me.'

'Please wear the condom,' says Andy. 'I want there to be something separating you and my girlfriend.'

'Fuck off, Andy,' she tells him, sweetly.

My heart's beating fast as I reach down to feel her hole with my finger. I have an unfamiliar fear. My cock is like a steel bar, so that's not the worry this time. It's that my desire for this girl is so strong, there's a danger I'll lose control in an unbull-like way as soon as I'm inside her. I try to tell myself she's just another hot woman who needs to be fucked by a stud, but I can't believe it.

Putting my cock inside her is like stepping into a hot bath. It's as if my whole body is enveloped by her. Her cunt holds my cock in a warm embrace. I mustn't think about how I'm feeling. I would like to make love to her, and maybe I will one day. Right now, I have to give her the fuck she expects from her nasty boyfriend.

Grabbing her wrists, I pin them to the pillow behind her head. She looks up at me with excited eyes as she pretends to struggle. 'You're too strong for me,' she says, breathlessly. 'I'll have to let you do whatever you want to me.'

'Yes, you will,' I say, thrusting into her five times, as hard as I can. It makes her gasp. I release her arms and dig my fingers into her breasts, leaving purple marks on her pale skin as I squeeze and twist them.

'You bastard!' she hisses.

'You love it, dirty bitch,' I tell her, with a sneer, as I thrust into her again with full force.

Her arms are still behind her head. It's out of character to be affectionate, but I can't help myself. I kiss her armpits, enjoying the hints of her sweat which push through the deodorant and perfume.

I realize I'm focusing on me again. I look into her face, watching for signs, as I move my cock back and forth in a steady rhythm. I *must* give her the best cum of her life.

Jenna again shows her flair for the unexpected. 'My cunt's only good enough for a beta male like Andy,' she says. 'You deserve better.'

She jerks her crotch backwards, disengaging her cunt from my cock, and rolls over. I'm confronted with the exquisite curve of her ass. I take a look at her bedside table, but can't see any oils or creams that would serve as lube. 'Spread your legs,' I tell her. 'Wide as you can. Show me both your slutty holes.'

I use two fingers to scoop Jenna's juices out of her cunt and smear them on her asshole. I want to make it slippery, but not too much. We both want this to hurt a little. I position myself on top of her. Breaking character for a moment, I whisper in her ear, 'Tell me if it's too much.' She nods.

I'm not *so* experienced at this, but I still find Jenna's tight little hole with my cock tip first time. I hold the base of my cock to stop it sliding off course and drive it slowly into her. The heat and tightness of Jenna's asshole is like nothing I've experienced before. Again, I'm faced with the danger of cumming too quickly. I calm myself down as I work my dick deeper inside her. My movements are small, half an inch up and down, but they're having a big effect on her. She's breathing quickly and noisily. If I didn't know better, I'd say she was going to ….

'You've got your cock up my arse, you fucker,' she says.

'The only hole you've got that's worth fucking,' I tell her.

This is a blatant lie, but she responds with an ecstatic, 'Oh, yeah!'

What I'm doing is having all the right effects, so I don't change anything. I keep prodding the core of her ass gently with my cock. Pushing her groin upward to get even more of me inside her, she lets out a groan which comes from the heart of her. Her whole body tenses. My cock feels like it's in a vice. It hurts, but I don't care. 'Fuck! Fuck! *Fuck!*' she screams, as an orgasm surges through her body.

As she relaxes, I'm in shock. I've never made a woman cum this way before. I pull out of her slowly. She turns over, looking equally surprised. Her pussy is in front of me. I want to lick it until she cums again. I could happily spend all night giving her pleasure. But she says, 'I want *you* to cum now.' Looking up at Andy, she adds, 'Both of you.'

This is the moment when I'd usually crouch beside her and let her jerk my cock until I covered her tits or belly. But not this time.

I look at Andy, who nods toward Jenna's cunt. I'm pleased to see this. It's an acknowledgement that, as the alpha male in the room, I belong there. But this is the real world, and there's somewhere else I have to go first. 'Bathroom?' I say. They both point to a door at the side of the room. I run there as fast as I can and close the door behind me. What I have to do isn't sexy. There's a bottle of liquid soap by the basin in their bathroom. I squirt some into my hand and rub it all over my cock and balls. I rinse them under the cold tap. I'm hoping this will desensitize my cock and increase my staying power.

Opening the door again, I find Jenna and Andy lying on the bed together, kissing and talking. 'I let another man put his dick up my arse,' she says. 'I've never let *you* do that.'

This is exactly what I was rushing to avoid. I've seen this too often with Paula and Ray. When a couple's discussing what they've done and what a bad girl she's been, they often want to be alone. This can be the moment for the bull to slip quietly away.

But when Jenna sees me, she spreads her legs, and pats the space between them. Kneeling up between her thighs, I lift her right leg and rest it on my lap. I shuffle forward and feed my cock into her pussy. Her vagina is glistening wetly and still wide from the last time I was inside her, but, even so, I feel the walls of her cunt gentle but firm around my cock.

Andy positions himself on the bed next to Jenna's head. She grabs his cock, puts it in her mouth, and moves her head back and forth. Looking at them, I feel almost jealous that she's doing this for him. Then I remember where *my* cock is and tell myself I have nothing to complain about.

I move inside her. If she looks like cumming again, I'll make sure it happens, but I feel my own moment approaching. I catch

Andy's eye. I feel a curiously strong connection with him. He and I are a team, working to reach a common goal.

I reach the point of no return sooner than I'd like. I tense my muscles in the hope of prolonging the moment, but I have no choice but to empty my seed into Jenna's cunt. Andy cums in her mouth at the same time.

He and I pull out of our respective holes and sit back on our ankles. We look at Jenna. She opens her mouth wide, showing us both how full of cum it is. Andy has nothing to be ashamed of there. She closes her mouth. There's a movement in her throat. Opening her mouth again, she sticks out her tongue, as if proving she's a good fiancée who swallows all of her man's seed.

This is strange for me to see. Normally, the woman would take the *bull*'s cum in her mouth and show her partner she'd swallowed it. Whatever sort of relationship I end up having with Jenna and Andy, it's not going to follow all the standard rules of cuckoldry. I won't have it all my own way.

Jenna's head slumps back on the pillow. Her eyes are closed. Her mouth is slightly open. The untrained person might check she's okay. But I've seen this before. It's the stupor of a woman who's finally been fucked properly. I can't take all the credit. Andy has played his part. It seems having *two* men pleasuring her did not disappoint.

She pats the bed on either side of her, inviting us both to lie down. As soon as all three heads are on the pillow, she turns to kiss me, pushing her tongue into my mouth. Maybe she thinks it's only fair that I taste Andy's cock.

I hope she's not going to experience too bad a drop now the excitement of the scene has faded. I don't want her to say, 'That was wrong. We can never do it again. Andy, I hope you can forgive me. Daniel, get out and never contact us again.'

She looks at me and asks, 'Any chance of round two before bedtime?'

I'm not so worried now that she's about to tell me to get out. Andy looks at me. 'Thank you,' he says. Cucks have thanked me for fucking their women before but, even so, I give him an inquiring look. 'See how happy she is,' he says, by way of explanation.

Jenna changes the subject. 'Anyone else hungry?'

'I could eat,' I say.

'Shall I see if I can get a table at the Shanghai Lounge?' suggests Andy, before adding quickly, 'Do you like Chinese, Daniel?'

'Love it,' I assure him.

He takes his phone out of his pocket and searches for the number. 'I suppose I'd better get used to booking a table for three,' he says, with a smile.

I'm happy with the way it's all turned out. Nevertheless, there is a part of me that wants to go back on everything I've said and leave. At the moment, I can't see a single flaw in Jenna. But she is human. As I get to know her better, inevitably I'll find things I don't like. I know I said I didn't find perfection interesting, but I've changed my mind. Everything that's happened so far tells me that Jenna is perfect *for me*. If I go now, she'll stay that way in my mind forever.

But I watch her getting ready to go out, unselfconsciously putting on a fresh pair of panties and looking through the dresses in her wardrobe, and I know I'm not going anywhere. I want this woman in my life for a long time. I thought this realization might frighten me, but it turns out the opposite is true. My cock is at its full size again. I stand up and ask Jenna, 'Do we have to head off immediately, or do we have time …?'

She turns and grins as she sees the state I'm in. 'Oh yes,' she says, walking toward me. 'We've got time.'

Rob Matthews was born in London. He divides his time between Britain and the United States. He lives with his wife Tina and their dog Boris. He is the author of *A Cuckold Odyssey - Come Home With Us*, *I Can Do It Better*, *We Make Our Own Rules*, and *I'm The One You Need*. He's also written the Interracial Cuckold Tales - *Black and Blue* and *Talking Bull*. Coming soon: the standalone *Cuckold Begins*. Follow Rob on Facebook and Twitter: www.facebook.com/robertpatrickmatthews @robandtina1